**"I'm taking care of Sophie out of obligation, nothing more. I owe it to my sister and her baby to do a good job. That's as far as it goes."**

"You could have fooled me."

Looking agitated, Hunter took another quick drink. "How do you intend to be a mom and get your PhD at the same time?"

Amanda looked aside and shook her head. "It's not something I need to work out just now, but I've always said where there's a will there's a way. And kids feel the love no matter what, when it's genuine."

"I didn't feel that from my own parents."

She knew exactly what he meant. "But that doesn't have to be the case with your own kids."

"Not going to have any, remember?"

She wanted to dig her fingers into her hair and scream. Why couldn't he see what a wonderful job he'd done taking care of Sophie?

# ASSIGNMENT: BABY

BY
LYNNE MARSHALL

MILLS & BOON®
Pure reading pleasure™

All the characters in this book have no existence outside the imagination
of the author, and have no relation whatsoever to anyone bearing the
same name or names. They are not even distantly inspired by any
individual known or unknown to the author, and all the incidents are
pure invention.

First published in Great Britain 2009
Harlequin Mills & Boon Limited,
Eton House, 18-24 Paradise Road, Richmond, Surrey TW9 1SR

© Lynne Marshall 2009

ISBN: 978 0 263 86834 0

Set in Times Roman 10¼ on 12¾ pt
03-0309-51643

Printed and bound in Spain
by Litografia Rosés, S.A., Barcelona

**Lynne Marshall** has been a Registered Nurse in a large California hospital for twenty-five years. She has now taken the leap to writing full time, but still volunteers at her local community hospital. After writing the book of her heart in 2000, she discovered the wonderful world of Medical™ Romance, where she feels the freedom to write the stories she loves. She is happily married, has two fantastic grown children, and a socially challenged rescued dog. Besides her passion for writing Medical™ Romance, she loves to travel and read. Thanks to the family dog, she takes long walks every day!

**Recent titles by the same author:**

PREGNANT NURSE, NEW-FOUND FAMILY
SINGLE DAD, NURSE BRIDE
IN HIS ANGEL'S ARMS
HER L.A. KNIGHT

This book is dedicated to the "Jack Howling" of my life—Sweet William. Here's to twenty-five more years!

# CHAPTER ONE

AMANDA DUNLAP prayed this wasn't fate's idea of a practical joke. It was the first day of her six-week statistical study on preventive cardiac care, which would comprise her first medical journal article. And there they were, the twenty carefully selected patients, each with three or four of the risk factors contributing to future heart disease—ticking time bombs, as her mentor had put it.

The participants sat quietly conversing amongst themselves, thumbing through the Mending Hearts Club syllabus and class outline, waiting for the evening to begin.

She glanced at her watch and a flutter of panic winged through her chest. After three months preparing every aspect of the curriculum for the pilot project, her bank account and her career were both on the line. If she achieved her patient goals, Los Angeles Mercy Hospital would use her health modification model for all three California Mercy hospitals, and her goal of a PhD in nursing would be waiting over the horizon. If she failed, she'd be stuck doing employee physicals and walk-in visits at the Serena Vista Clinic—and proving her parents right that she was reaching beyond her capabilities.

Yesterday, just her luck, all plans had come to a screeching halt when her mentor had dropped out for personal health reasons. Without a doctor to lend his name to the already promised medical journal article, her proverbial nurse practitioner butt was in a sling.

Thank heavens the Mercy Hospital medical director had found a replacement for their satellite clinic. Only one problem remained.

Where was her hero?

While destiny snickered, Amanda checked her watch again—seven-ten. Perhaps the replacement had gotten lost on the drive in or was wandering around trying to find the patient education classrooms? Whatever the reason for tardiness, she'd be forgiving, but she couldn't wait a second longer. Having every minute of her two-hour introductory class mapped out, she owed it to the participants to keep her promise of starting and ending the sessions on time.

"Good evening, I'm Amanda Dunlap," she said, and waited for everyone to face forward and quiet down. "I'm so happy to see all of you here tonight." She went on to explain the purpose of the class.

A scuffle at the back of the room drew her attention from the faces in the front row. She glanced up in time to see the door swing open. An empty infant car seat was wedged to hold it open. Next a diaper bag was tossed into the back of the room, soon followed by a masculine thigh and shoulder pushing through.

A gurgling baby faced outward in a special carrier strapped across a man's chest, drawing Amanda's immediate attention. The child wore bright pink overalls and a patterned top, with super-white mock sports shoes made especially for feet that didn't yet walk.

Amanda automatically grinned, and sweet warmth trickled throughout her body at the sight. Her substitute mentor was not only a hero but also a family man.

During her brief marriage, after never having had a maternal thought in her life, she'd missed a period, thought she'd been pregnant, and discovered a secret even she'd never suspected. She wanted a baby. Her husband had been thrown into a tailspin when she'd brought up the possibility. When it had turned out she wasn't pregnant, her heart had already changed forever.

Now she didn't know if she'd be able to have a baby of her own. She glanced at the bittersweet surprise popping through the door and gave a wan smile.

Her eyes drifted upward to the bearer of the bright pink baby package, and her breath stuck in her throat. She froze, and grappled to maintain her composure as a chill ran up her spine.

Hunter.

She hadn't seen him in three years.

Bracing herself at the lectern until her knuckles went white, she recognized the sculpted cheekbones and the long jaw. Had he broken his nose?

Under thick, fox-brown hair and a strong brow were piercing though slightly apologetic brown eyes. They crinkled at the corners and his familiar mouth slipped into a tentative half smile. He followed it with a cautious nod.

Anxiety burst free in her chest, sending her heart into a gallop. She evened out her breathing and waited for her pulse to calm while continuing her death grip on the stand.

Hunter Phillips.

Fast as fireworks, thoughts exploded through her mind. She wanted to cry and point at his baby. *That's what I wanted and you wouldn't let me have it!*

When they'd married, they'd both agreed to pursue their careers at the expense of having children. Hunter's parents had done a grand job of ignoring him and his sister in favor of their professions, and he'd vowed never to repeat their mistakes.

Amanda had accepted his conditions, since she had wanted to become a nurse practitioner and one day achieve her doctorate in nursing.

After her missed period and the newfound desire to be a mother, she'd pressed him on the topic. He'd accused her of being so wrapped up in work and school that she'd be too busy to care for a houseplant, let alone a child. That had stung to her core, and it still hurt to recall his lack of confidence in her. Just like her parents…

She stared at the gurgling baby. He'd moved on, found someone else and had the family he'd told her he'd never in a million years want. Pain seared her side as if he'd stabbed her. Could Hunter be so cruel? She thinned her lips and tried to hide the sadness coiling in her heart.

Moisture prickled in her eyes. Feeling betrayed, she bit back emotion, swallowed hard and forced her face into a professional expression, praying that somehow she'd make it through the night. Then, first thing tomorrow morning, she'd call the medical director and demand a new mentor. She'd wing it by herself, work doubly hard—whatever it took until he found another replacement. No way would she work with Hunter.

She shook her head. Unbelievable as it was, her savior had turned out to be her ex-husband, in a wrinkled business suit with a bright pink baby surprise strapped to his chest.

Everyone in the classroom watched and waited. She couldn't stand there dumbfounded for one more second, so she took a deep breath to introduce him.

Oh, God.

"Good evening, everyone. Sorry I'm late," Hunter said, realizing they were all staring at him and Mandy hadn't yet been able to make her mouth work.

With everyone watching, he bent to pick up the baby carrier and almost bumped heads with Sophie. Could things get any more awkward? Even though he'd rehearsed and prepared for this moment the entire drive over, the depth of pain at seeing her again almost took his breath away.

After three years of hell and soul-searching since their divorce, the last thing he'd wanted to do was face her again under these unusual circumstances. But it seemed there was no way out. If he didn't help Mandy, the class would be history. And though he wasn't sure what her stake in it was, he was certain of his motivation.

Joel Hersh, the man who'd made sure Hunter had gotten a staff position at Mercy Hospital after his residency, had contacted him just that morning.

"You've heard about Charles Beiderman?" Joel had said.

"Yeah. Poor guy. And so unexpected." He'd been diagnosed with lymphoma.

"Charles was set to mentor one of our nurse practitioners on a community outreach program at our Serena Vista Clinic," Dr. Hersh had gone on to explain in detail.

"Sounds interesting."

"Yes, her approach to reaching patients long before they require surgical cardiac intervention is the way of the future. Wouldn't you agree?"

"Absolutely. Preventive care is the best offense." If only his father had thought the same, maybe his stroke could have been averted.

"I'm in a bind. The patients have already been lined up and everything is set to go. It would be cost-effective if you stepped in."

It was the first favor Joel had ever asked of Hunter. "Hey, I'd be glad to help," he said, straightening his tie. Since his father's recent death, he'd made it a personal goal to enlighten his patients about blood pressure and heart health. This would be an opportunity to reach more people.

"Good, then. I'll let Amanda know she can proceed with the study."

His shoulders had stiffened at the name. "Amanda?"

"Yes. Amanda Dunlap."

Hunter's heart had stumbled. His fingers had clutched the knot in his tie just above the similar knot that had formed in his throat. Mandy? As in his ex-wife, Mandy? Obviously the medical director didn't know. This couldn't have come at a worse time for him, but he couldn't very well weasel out now. And he did owe the man a major favor…

Now, placing the carrier on a nearby table, Hunter looked around the room filled with middle-aged faces, ignoring the painful reminder at the head. "Don't mind me." He waved his hand, pretending to have everything under control, while still reeling from the earthquake in his gut at seeing Mandy again. If he felt this shaken up, he could only imagine what must be going through *her* mind. "Go right ahead."

"Class, this is my ex-hu…er…Dr. Phillips," Mandy said, with a corrected businesslike tone. She blushed crimson at her near mistake, which turned her blue eyes almost neon and softened the effect of her curt introduction. Obviously she was no happier to see him than he was to be here.

He'd missed those fiery eyes, even though they looked boggled right about now, as though she'd just been caught out on reality TV. He could only imagine how he must look.

"We were getting ready to have a quick anatomy class on the heart," she said, obviously trying to hide her true reaction to his showing up in *her* classroom. "Why don't you do the honors?"

He fought the urge to glance over his shoulder, point to his own chest and mouth, *Me?* Instead, he forced an affable smile and said, "Sure." She'd put him on the spot and given him no choice.

He could handle this. No problem. He glanced around wondering where to put the baby carrier, planning to buckle Sophie inside. That was if he could remember how to set it up outside of the car.

Sophie gurgled and cooed. One of the women students sprang up. "I'll hold her. I've got seven grandchildren."

"Oh," he said, relieved. "Thanks."

She lifted the child from the harness around his chest. As naturally as a penguin sheltering its young, she took the baby into her arms and grinned at her. Sophie didn't seem to mind, so he nodded in gratitude.

As he approached the front of the class, Mandy rolled a cart to the center of the room for his use. Perched on top sat a larger-than-life plastic heart complete with arteries. She'd wasted no time getting him involved. Was this the price he had to pay for being late?

Doing a quick mental review of heart physiology, he stepped forward. He remembered the absurd harness and fought clumsily to remove it. After running his hand through his hair and straightening his shirt and jacket, he jumped right in on the mini anatomy lesson. He used his penlight as a pointer and made sound effects to explain the role of circulation and heart valves. *Lub-dub. Thump-swish.*

Sophie appeared fascinated.

Ten minutes later, Mandy cleared her throat…several times. He glanced up, stopped his long-winded lecture and noticed her squinting and nodding toward the students. Following the roll of her eyes, he saw the dazed look on everyone's faces. Had he moved beyond layman's terms? Possibly. At least it had kept his mind off his ex-wife for a while.

"Yes, well…that will be enough anatomy for today. Mandy? I mean, Ms. Dunlap, what's next?"

With a subtle sigh of relief, she snatched up her notes and stepped to the podium, cutting in front of him. She still wore the same fragrance—some aromatherapy herbal body lotion. Inhaling, he didn't feel inclined to step away, but he backed up just enough to give her room. She turned and glanced at him briefly before addressing the class. He averted his gaze rather than chance her seeing the surprising and pathetic hope he still harbored. Was he really such a glutton for punishment? He studied her dark brunette hair. She'd pulled the thick and shiny waves into her signature low ponytail, complete with long escaped strands around the ears.

Some things hadn't changed about Mandy. Except now she looked borderline too thin, as if she'd been working hard and long and not caring for herself enough. So what else was new? When they'd been married they'd watched over each other, balancing out their tendencies toward personal neglect in favor of work.

Mandy tossed another warning stare over her shoulder. Okay. He got it. Trying hard to seem aloof and casual, he strode toward Sophie and, when the grandmotherly student offered, took the baby back. It was all a paltry show to prove he wasn't the least bit shaken up about seeing Mandy. Now, if he could only convince himself…

The nine-month-old baby kicked her legs several times and squealed with glee. He quieted her down with a pacifier he dug out of his pocket, and found a seat at the back of the class with an excellent view of his ex-wife.

He'd known it would be difficult, but still he hadn't expected to be this jarred by seeing her again. He'd spent a full year trying to put the pieces of his life back together after their breakup. How could she have walked away over a disagreement on kids? Why had he let her? He'd moped, drunk too much, even womanized briefly. Nothing had helped until he'd toughened up and gone back to the way of his parents: becoming a devoted workaholic. It hadn't changed anything, but at least it had kept him from thinking about her. His gaze drifted upward to the woman he'd once loved and trusted—until she'd changed their game plan.

The topic turned to the importance of daily exercise. Mandy had everyone up and stretching. Hunter had a sudden memory of being in running gear with her. She'd worn a sports bra and silky short-shorts with slits up the sides. A lazy smile crossed his lips. Damn, he was a masochist.

"We'll be doing this routine every morning. Isn't that right, Dr. Phillips?"

What? He straightened in his chair and tried to appear halfway alert. "I'm sorry. I was distracted with the baby."

"Class, you can all sit down." Clearly giving him the benefit of the doubt, she gave a tolerant nod, but he detected something else in her eyes. "I was saying that after thorough physical examinations, we'll be evaluating everyone here and dividing them into groups of walkers and joggers. I'll handle the walkers and…" She glanced at Hunter and frowned. "Well, we'll figure that out later."

Hmm. He would play along for now, but once class was over, and he had Mandy to himself, he'd grill her on what exactly *was* expected of him and for how many hours a day. Since Joel Hersh had handily omitted those details. And if his suspicions were right that she planned to replace him, he'd put his foot down. As difficult as it would be, he owed his father and Joel at least that much.

He would have spent more time thinking about his Mending Hearts Club duties, but Sophie had a hold of his nose. She twisted it in an unnatural direction. When he looked up, for the first time that night a smile hinted at the corners of Mandy's mouth. Until now she'd been ignoring them both. Settling for any possible headway, and feeling like the class clown, he shrugged, gingerly removed Sophie's sticky fingers, and apologized with a smile. Looking flustered, Mandy reached for a loose lock of hair and nodded, before quickly looking away.

As the class went on, he surreptitiously read part of the syllabus—as much as was possible with Sophie trying her best to swat at the pages and rip them to shreds. Mandy had everything carefully analyzed and set up to perfection. To do anything less would go against her character.

An hour and a half later, the room had cleared of everyone but Mandy, Sophie and Hunter.

She tugged at her hair again and approached cautiously, slowly building speed and looking more confident. "No way are we going to work together," she said.

"Yes, way. Because I've signed on and I'm not a quitter."

"I'm calling Dr. Hersh first thing tomorrow morning and asking for a replacement."

"And he'll tell you exactly what he told me. 'Good thing you've agreed, Hunter. I was about to cancel the class.'"

After a brief, silent standoff, she said, "I don't believe you."

"It's true, so get over it. I'm here to stay." One little white lie couldn't possibly hurt their already strained partnership.

Mandy stared him down with a defiant glint in her eyes.

"I'm your last resort. Take it or leave it," he said.

Something changed in her demeanor. Was it acceptance of her rotten luck?

She walked back to the podium and shuffled some papers. "I almost had a heart attack when you walked into the room."

Hunter followed her. "Then you were in the right class."

"Don't be a smart-ass," she said.

"Believe me, no one was more surprised than I when Joel told me who I'd be working with."

"Why did you agree to work with me?"

"Because you needed help," he said quietly.

She glanced at him, but her eyes darted away before he could engage her.

Feeling a twinge of guilt, he continued. "That's not completely true." He scratched the back of his neck. "I didn't know you were involved until I'd already committed."

She tilted her head and quirked her mouth, looking neither disappointed nor surprised at his confession. "But you didn't back out?"

"Nope."

She shook her head. They stared at each other for a beat, and he thought he saw a hint of gratitude.

Drawing her brows together, she gazed at Sophie and asked with an acerbic flare, "Babysitter problems?"

The baby had fallen asleep halfway through the session, and had used his shoulder to lay her head and drool on.

"No. This is Jade's daughter. I *am* the babysitter."

"Jade had a baby?" Relief flashed on her face but she quickly concealed it. Amanda and Jade had become great friends while she and Hunter had been married. Unfortunately, after the divorce they'd drifted apart. Her shoulders relaxed and she seemed to breathe easier. "How wonderful."

A surge of dread coursed through him. Of course—how else would it look? *You jerk!* What a heel she must have thought he was. "Oh, man, you thought Sophie was mine, didn't you?"

She looked confused. "What was I supposed to think, Hunter?"

A sudden need to make sure she knew and understood

his circumstances made him blurt out, "For the record, I'm not remarried or involved, and I don't have any children."

She lifted her brows, and after a long silence said, "I can't believe Jade had a baby."

"It wasn't under the best circumstances. She's a single mother and she's been having a rough time of it since delivery. Truth is, she's admitted herself to the hospital for treatment for severe postpartum depression, and I'm Sophie's guardian for at least the next month."

She looked him square in the face and he noticed a flicker of surprise in her eyes. "All the more reason for you to step down and let me find someone else…"

"We've gone over that already, Mandy."

Subtle warmth spread across his chest. When he placed a hand on his shirt, he realized with chagrin that Sophie needed a diaper change. Now.

"Oh, damn," he said, holding the baby at a distance and letting the overflow drip to the floor. He'd have to send the suit to the cleaners. He was still on a learning curve with diapers— and *everything* else where his niece was concerned. Apparently he hadn't sealed the diaper tight enough.

Sophie's eyes opened and she fussed, fisted her hand and shoved it into her mouth. He strode to the nearby table and reached for the diaper bag, then dug inside with one hand while balancing the baby under his other arm, butt out and away from his suit. The diaper bag dropped to the floor. "Damn it."

From the podium, Mandy shook her head and rolled her eyes. "Here, let me help you out."

If he didn't love Jade so much, he would never have agreed to take on such a responsibility. What was he supposed to do with a baby? But, through their parents' neglect, the bond between him and his sister had been cemented. He couldn't let her down.

Mandy approached, picked up the bag, reached inside and tossed him a cloth diaper and some baby wipes. After spreading out the small vinyl-lined diaper-changing pad on the floor, she reached for Sophie, who continued to protest. Mandy gently patted the baby's head to help soothe her. "There, there. We'll get you fixed up in no time so you can go back to sleep."

The craziest thought occurred to him: he was thankful the baby didn't have a diaper rash—as though it would reflect badly on his parenting skills. All three and a half days of them.

He couldn't believe he still cared what Mandy thought, or that he was having such a mundane moment with the woman he'd never been able to get completely out of his system. Be careful, he warned himself. She can't be trusted.

He'd stood still too long, and let things grow too quiet. She glanced up at him with questioning aqua eyes.

"So you're working toward your PhD, I'm told."

"Who told you?"

"Dr. Hersh. He seems very impressed with this study of yours." Maybe she'd thrown herself back into her career and had given up on her baby fantasy?

She smiled. Sophie fussed again.

"I think she's hungry," she said. "Did you bring a bottle?"

He finished wiping his hands and removed his soiled jacket, wishing he could strip off his shirt, too. Mandy had always been so organized. Even now, when it was none of her concern, she seemed to know exactly what needed to be done. "Uh, yes. There's a can of powdered formula and a bottle of water to mix it with somewhere in there."

"You take care of the meal and I'll change her diaper. Did you bring her jammies?"

"Jammies?" He paused. "Oh, pajamas. Yes."

"Let me guess. Pink ones?" She smiled briefly and he

thought daylight had broken through the night. Her finely pointed features had never ceased to amaze him, and right now the slant of her eyes and the turn of her nose captivated him. Through his eyes, Mandy had always been beautiful, and it appeared she'd only gotten better with time. But what was the point of entertaining those thoughts?

He glanced at his niece on the changing pad. How ironic. Mandy's sudden desire to have a baby had driven them apart. Now a helpless baby was forcing them to drop the past and focus on the "right now."

He needed to say something. Anything. Now. "Jade has this thing for pink…for such a staunch feminist it's strange…" he mumbled, and fumbled with the can.

"Pink is just a color, not a political statement." She looked up, a tentative look in her eyes. "She's really a beautiful baby."

"You think?" Truth was he didn't have a clue how babies were supposed to look.

"How old is she?"

"Uh…nine months."

Mandy kept staring at him, and he felt compelled to fill the silence. "Who'd have thought in a million years we'd be working together again?"

"If I can finagle it, we *won't* be working together."

He finally popped open the powdered formula can. "I told you—it's a done deal," he said. "Baby and all."

Amanda pondered the incongruity of their current situation. When they'd married, they'd agreed to put their careers first and forever. And because she'd worked so hard the stress had caused her to miss a period. The fleeting possibility of being pregnant had changed her outlook on babies so drastically she'd known she could no longer agree to a life without children.

Even though she hadn't turned out to be pregnant, she'd already made that choice. She wanted a family, not just a degree. But Hunter hadn't budged. *"You promised you never wanted children,"* he had repeated, over and over.

"Life is certainly full of surprises," she said under her breath now, as she removed the soiled disposable diaper, thinking she couldn't have made up a wilder story if she'd tried. She and Hunter working together while he took care of his niece? She shook her head. "Speaking of surprises, you'll need to actually read my syllabus if you insist on being my mentor."

He nodded. "I know. And I will."

"I've got everything broken down day by day," she said, trying her hardest not to think about how wonderful it felt to hold a real live baby in her arms. "Like I said, we'll start with physical examinations tomorrow. I've arranged for two exam rooms on the first floor. You can do the men and I'll do the women." She concentrated on Sophie, cleaning her porcelain fine skin with a moist baby wipe, trying not to succumb to her charm. "We need to get labs drawn and EKGs."

Back then all she'd wanted was Hunter and a baby…and an advanced degree. Was that too much to ask? And here they were.

"We'll do stress tests on Thursday, and by Friday we should have our group divided for the physical training portion." If only things could have been different. This could be their baby and they could be working as husband and wife… Where was she now? She didn't dare look into his eyes.

"Oh, and you'll have to follow the diet while you're involved. I know how you like your double-double cheeseburgers, but that's out of the question for now."

He nodded while fiddling with the formula can and half-heartedly measuring out a scoop for the bottle. "As far as my eating is concerned, you've got me all wrong. Since Dad died from a stroke I've opted to change the one thing I have control over. My diet."

"I'm so sorry to hear about your father, Hunter. Did you ever have a chance to work things out?"

He somberly shook his head.

Amanda had finished the diaper change and now sat yoga-style. Hunter attempted to join her and almost spilled the formula. His knees were high off the floor and his back was hunched awkwardly. Completely unnatural, and obviously in pain, there he sat. She tried not to think how silly he looked, and almost felt sorry for him. Almost.

Without being asked, Amanda took the scoop from his hands and read the label. Sophie, tired of playing with her toes, rolled over and crawled across the floor.

Amanda mixed the powdered formula into the water and studied Hunter. Why not state the obvious? "It'll be tough working together." She sighed. "But we're adults, Hunter. And if you insist on staying, I'll just have to get used to it."

Shaking the bottle, Amanda tried to get Sophie's attention. When the baby noticed, she immediately crawled over and sat. She grabbed the bottle with both hands and stuck it into her mouth. Amanda tried not to react to how cute that was. Glancing at Hunter, she noticed an apathetic glaze in his eyes. Obviously his mind was elsewhere, and he was no more inter-ested in babies today than he'd been when they were married.

It being tough to work together was the understatement of the century. Mandy watched him with her sea-blue eyes and he re-membered how he'd never gotten tired of looking at her when they were a couple. Being around her day after day would be torture.

He wished that things hadn't gone so sour between them. But, like she'd said earlier, life was full of surprises. Like when she'd had a sudden change of heart about wanting babies. Both being young and stubborn to a fault, and compromise being a foreign word, they had foolishly lost everything.

And here they were.

She stood up and dusted her hands on her workout pants. His knees cracked when he joined her. Her pants seemed baggy. She clapped her hands together and stared him smack in the face.

"Have you lost weight?"

"Did you break your nose?"

They asked the questions in unison.

"Yes."

They shared an awkward moment at having spoken at the same time twice. Eyeing each other suspiciously, they let their respective questions lie for another time.

Sophie dropped her bottle, crawled between them and slapped at Hunter's pant leg.

He picked her up. "It's way past her bedtime," he said, letting his gaze linger an extra moment on Mandy's face. Being this close put him off balance. "And I've got an hour's drive home."

She scratched her cheek and shifted her weight back and forth. "Right. Have you made childcare arrangements?"

He shook his head. "It's going to be traumatic enough for Sophie not to have Jade around. I can't bring myself to drop her off anywhere with strangers. My medical assistant and I have been working things out at the Mercy clinic."

She nodded and lifted her chin. "Then we'll just have to do our best to work around Sophie, too, I guess."

Their eyes locked in benign accord. "Thanks for understanding."

"No problem," she said, and quickly glanced down. "Jade was my friend, too."

But as far as Hunter was concerned, he did have a problem.

A major problem. The very thought of being around Mandy day in and day out, with all the memories, concerns and longings it would dig up, made the monumental task of single-handedly caring for Sophie feel like a mere stroll in the park.

# CHAPTER TWO

AMANDA glanced at the clock on the wall of the tightly packed office. Two desks had been crammed into a space that had once been an exam room. She and Hunter would be painfully close in here but would have to make do, since she'd go to any length for the heart study and her article. She could almost touch her dream, and if dealing with her ex-husband and all the baggage he brought with him was the price she'd have to pay to reach it, so be it.

Amanda had her reasons for advocating diet and exercise to avoid invasive procedures, and she'd put her nursing career on the line for the Mending Hearts Club program. Promoting holistic heart health was the best option, and nothing would stop her from moving forward as planned.

Not even Hunter.

Confronting Hunter last night had practically sent her into palpitations, and had come in a close second to the shock she'd felt after her recent diagnosis. Sure, they'd acted mature and civil toward one another, but the emotional storm raging beneath the surface of her carefully orchestrated facade had almost pulled her into its depths in the process.

Memories steamrollered through her mind. She remembered what a fine doctor he was, and how gentle he could be one moment, as well as how he could become an unsympathetic oaf the next. And she asked herself questions—questions about why they couldn't have handled their dilemma differently, like agreeing to postpone a baby discussion for another time instead of both getting swept up in a temperamental standoff. She'd made the mistake of thinking they were soul mates. That if she'd been the true love of his life he'd have done anything for her. But they'd been young and headstrong. And once the baby bug had bitten Amanda, their future had changed, whether Hunter had been ready to deal with the fact or not.

A never-ending parade of thoughts had kept her awake most of the night. And a tiny voice still kept wondering if maybe their marriage could have survived.

She didn't really know Hunter anymore. Their lives and circumstances had evolved, and now they were nothing more than business professionals working on the same project. But he'd made it clear he wasn't involved with anyone. Why would he do that with a mere project partner?

She stepped outside the second-floor office and tapped on the first door—a makeshift exam room that used to be a supply closet.

"Mrs. Anderson, are you ready for me yet?"

Mrs. Anderson was Amanda's second physical of the morning. Two of the male patients who had appointments with Hunter still sat down the hall, in a group waiting room.

"Yes. Come in." The patient's muffled voice could barely be heard.

Amanda's eyes drifted to her watch. He was late—again.

Though Hunter had been nearly a half hour late, due to bad traffic and a fussy baby, he'd made up for lost time. By mid-morning he and Mandy had gotten halfway through the physical examinations.

Thankfully, Sophie had played contentedly in a portable playpen in one tiny corner of the office. He liked to think the soft and relaxing classical music from his laptop made the difference. Out of desperation he'd put music on in the car on the drive to work, when Sophie had begun to wail shortly after they'd entered the freeway. The noise from her crying had jangled his nerves until his temples had throbbed. When she'd finally quieted down, he'd taken a long and deep breath of relief, though he still suffered from a dull headache.

From time to time in the office, Sophie let out a shrill noise, or banged a slobbery rubber toy until it squeaked. Over and over. Would he ever get used to being around a kid?

At the first outburst, Mandy had jumped in her seat and tossed her pen in surprise. He'd bitten back his urge to laugh at her. *Yeah, well, get used to it. This is the reality of a baby, sweetheart.*

Mandy looked even more tired than yesterday, as though she'd only gotten a few hours' sleep. Considering all that his guilty conscience had dredged up last night, about what he'd once said or done to Mandy, he'd managed to sleep fairly well. But packing up a child and commuting at the peak traffic hour had put him behind schedule again. Sophie hated being cooped up in a car seat, and made his life miserable with protest. This routine would grow stale quickly, but he'd do it—because he'd committed to Mandy and Dr. Hersh, and he owed them both. He owed it to his father, too.

Noticing the tension at the corners of Mandy's eyes, he wondered if their being forced to work together was such a good idea after all. Did either of them need to be reminded that they'd once shared a great love and blown it? And now he was dangling the baby she'd wanted all along right before her eyes.

"Here," he said. "I snagged you a cup of coffee from the employee lounge. You look like you need it."

"Oh, thanks. But you have it."

"You're saying no to coffee? Are you the same woman who used to savor that first cup every day?"

She gave a lifeless smile that didn't come close to her eyes. "Now I only do decaf."

That was certainly a change. Something wasn't right, and he had strong suspicions it had nothing to do with the coffee.

"Is something bothering you?" He took a sip rather than waste the drink.

"What? Oh, no." She reached for the stack of neatly piled charts on her desk and took the next one.

"You seem upset about something. It's me, isn't it?"

Her shoulders slumped and she stopped thumbing through the charts. "Men." She sighed. She thinned her lips and shook her head. "You're not the center of my universe, Hunter."

To lighten things up, he feigned a wound to the heart and waited for her to unwind a bit. "What is it, then? Is there something I can help you with?"

"Do you really need to know? We're nothing more than business associates. Remember?"

In other words…back off. Hunter nodded knowingly. "Gotcha." He reached for his next patient's chart and made some preliminary notes on the form to distract himself as Mandy's words echoed in his head. *We're nothing more than business associates.*

By lunchtime they'd each performed ten physicals. Amanda hoped she could set up the participants with the overnight halter monitors quickly. She wanted to leave early to rest a bit before her Urgent Care duty, which began at seven. Hunter had told her he had a late-afternoon clinic scheduled back at Mercy Hospital.

In light of her recent diagnosis, she knew she needed to stay calm and get more rest, but life wasn't exactly cooperating. She'd had palpitations a couple of times already this morning, and couldn't afford to keep feeling so stressed. If she didn't watch out she would wind up back in the ER. And then where would her Mending Hearts Club program be?

And Hunter. How was she supposed to handle working with him every day, pretending she was fine with it, and that her heart didn't still have a gaping wound where he was concerned? The smell of his aftershave reminded her how, when they'd first broken up, she'd bought his brand and sniffed it like potpourri. Then cried until her nose was congested and she couldn't smell anymore. How pitiful was that?

Amanda sat at her desk, cradling her forehead in her hands. Sophie was quiet, and Amanda had been so wrapped up in her thoughts she'd forgotten the baby was even there. Was that treating her like a houseplant? She glanced into the playpen. Sophie had fallen asleep; no wonder she hadn't noticed her. The nap probably had to do with the soothing nocturne now playing on Hunter's laptop. Too bad it hadn't helped her headache.

"There's nothing like Chopin's piano pieces to massage the nerves." Hunter's distinct masculine voice as he entered the room made Amanda gasp and jerk her head up. "I'm sorry," he said. "I didn't mean to startle you."

"I'm just a bit edgy," she said. "I don't recall you being a Chopin man."

"You're looking at the new and improved version of me."

"Yeah? Well, for the record, I liked your old nose better." Why did his mere presence make her feel so testy?

Taking her rebuke in his stride, Hunter sat and hitched half his mouth into a smile, then rubbed the bump on the bridge of his nose. "Yeah? Well, I got it defending myself against a gang of hoodlums."

"Really?" she said flatly.

"Must have been a dozen of them. Came at me from all angles."

"Uh-huh." His efforts at lightening her mood failed miserably.

"And they were huge."

She avoided looking at him, fearing she might crack a smile.

After a moment, he rolled his chair next to hers. He had that *I've-been-thinking* look in his eyes.

When they'd been married, and they'd had a problem to solve, he'd withdraw for anywhere from a few hours to a few days—then suddenly resurface with that exact expression to present his fail-safe plan. The problem was, she'd rarely agreed with his solutions.

Well, here he was beside her, looking that way again, and she wondered what great insight he was about to share.

"I've been thinking," he said.

She almost smiled.

He touched her hand with one finger, causing an unwanted spark of warmth on the underside of her wrist.

He gave an understanding nod. "This *is* a bizarre situation, given our history, but if we keep reminding ourselves it's strictly a professional association, things should work out. I admit that seeing you has been a shock, and you've admitted it was the same for you, but we'll get used to being around each other again." He rested his hand on hers and looked into her eyes. She blinked. "Let's just keep focused on why we're here. This is for Joel and my father—and whatever reason you're working so passionately for."

She'd resisted that tingle at first contact by tricking herself into thinking it was a fluke. Her hand had been cold, and that was why she'd felt it. That was all. But now, with his hand on top of hers, the unsettled feeling made her want to squirm. The touch crept up the surface of her skin as if a cool breath tickled the inside of her elbow. It had been hard enough facing him after years of separation; now, adding this innocent touch, it all felt far too intimate. She couldn't let herself go there.

"Mandy, you're not the only one feeling all mixed up."

"I realize that," she said, removing her hand and diverting her eyes. Had he read her mind?

When had they changed places? Wasn't she the one who'd used to initiate enlightening conversations and he who had given curt replies? Maybe his nose wasn't all that had changed.

Having a sudden need to move away from him, she reached for the intercom and asked the receptionist to send the first patient in for halter monitor application. While she waited, she continued to avoid his gaze by pretending to read the patient's chart. She couldn't decipher a single word.

"Hello, Mrs. Drake." Amanda stood and gestured for the patient to sit at the chair in front of her desk. "Are you ready to wear the halter all night?"

"Will it get really irritating when I try to sleep?"

"Maybe a little, but you'll survive."

"Okay, I'll give it a shot," the round, middle-aged lady replied cheerfully.

Amanda assisted the woman by applying the EKG leads after the patient had opened her blouse. She removed the monitor from its portable pocket and unwrapped the wires, before connecting it to the leads on Mrs. Drake, then she put the device back into its halter pocket for easy traveling. She'd analyze the findings tomorrow, along with all of the others.

Demonstrating his somewhat improved caregiver skills, Hunter removed Sophie's bottle of formula from the portable bottle warmer—which Mandy had helped him set up—and checked the contents for heat level on the inside of his wrist, as previously instructed by Mandy, before giving it to his niece. Amanda tried her best not to notice, but the office was so small.

While she received her next patient, and the baby gulped her meal, he quietly packed up all of his paraphernalia, picked up Sophie, and left the clinic without so much as a nod or a goodbye.

Amanda refused to be affected. Would she expect anything more from any other colleague? After all, she'd been busy with a patient. If Dr. Beiderman had become her mentor and had left without saying goodbye, would she feel slighted? Not at all. Business associates had schedules to keep regardless of social niceties. That was the frame of mind she must keep while dealing with Hunter—strictly professional.

So what was this empty feeling settling into the center of her chest? And why did the office seem so dead and lifeless now?

She shook her head, refusing to go down that old and familiar road. Instead, she decided that if she were going to survive the Mending Hearts Club program, she'd need rules. Rules to keep things in perspective. She called for her next patient and while she waited scribbled a short list, just like she used to do. She planned to run it by Hunter tomorrow.

Hunter tossed his briefcase on his desk, slid into the cushy leather chair and rubbed his neck. The freeway drive back to Mercy Hospital had been bumper to bumper, and Sophie had wailed most of the way. This time music hadn't calmed her down. He felt the tension right…*there*. Ah.

Thankfully Sophie had slept for the last part of the drive, but how long would she tolerate being cooped up in her car seat on a daily basis? And when he was finally able to contact Jade, how would he explain his three-hour round-trip commute? She would not approve.

If there'd been any way to avoid taking on his niece, he

would have suggested it. But Jade would never have considered leaving her baby with their mother, and Hunter would never expect her to. He ground his teeth, wishing Jade had at least one girlfriend she trusted as much as him.

For now his medical assistant, Maria, a short, plump woman with a gentle spirit, a contagious smile and a penchant for babies, had Sophie at her workstation while he prepared for his jam-packed afternoon clinic. He'd never be able to thank her enough. She bounced the baby on her knee until Hunter heard his niece's hearty belly laugh. It should have made him smile.

He bored a hole into the dark mahogany wood with his stare while he rubbed his temples and tried not to think about Mandy.

The commute had zapped his energy, too. Instinctively he reached for his earphones and plugged them in. He'd listen to Wagner's *Ride of the Valkyries* for a quick boost of energy.

Three months ago he'd taken Jade to music therapy for her depression. It hadn't helped her one iota, but through music he'd gotten in touch with his deepest feelings and, though shocking at first, had discovered his true gifts as a doctor.

The music therapy instructor had said he was a wounded healer, intuitive and caring. Yeah, he'd thought, with a wry smile, next he'd be reading his horoscope. Truth was, with the help of carefully chosen music, he'd noticed he could change Sophie's moods as much as his own. And if he could calm a baby down with music, wouldn't daily music and relaxation be beneficial for the heart study patients, too? He wondered if it might have helped his father.

Already Mandy's project mattered to him. He wanted to be useful, not a distraction for her. Maybe if she could put the past aside and see how sincere he was in wanting to help, they could pull this project off. But if their being thrown together felt one-tenth as hard for her as it did for him, he knew it wouldn't be easy.

Maria tapped on his door and, with Sophie contentedly resting on her hip, handed him his first afternoon appointment chart. She should be getting double salary for helping out, but after today he'd be out of the clinic until the Mending Hearts Club study was over, and she'd be working for Dr. Jimenez.

Fifteen minutes later, Hunter palpated his patient's left lower quadrant and determined that he no longer had tenderness from his diverticulitis flare-up. Last week the same patient had been doubled over in pain and begging to be hospitalized. A forty-eight-hour clear liquid diet and two different antibiotics had helped his condition miraculously in one short week.

He glanced at the patient's wife. She'd accompanied her husband last week for the visit, but Hunter had been totally preoccupied with his sick patient. He squinted, and looked at her again.

"Are you aware your thyroid is enlarged?" Why hadn't he noticed that slight asymmetry before?

Her hand flew to her neck, as if to check for herself.

"You can get dressed now," Hunter said to the man. "But take every single pill until they're gone, in order not to have rebound diverticulitis or to develop a drug-resistant strain of infection."

The patient nodded.

Hunter washed his hands. "Let me take a look," he said, turning to the wife.

Using his fingertips, he lightly palpated the area overlying her larynx and found a small but firm nodule. "Does this hurt?"

She shook her head, but alarm registered in her stare.

"Swallow?"

She complied. The nodule was fixed to the right lobe of the thyroid.

He felt for nearby enlarged lymph nodes, but didn't find any. A good sign. "Have you been feeling any different?"

"No."

"I'm going to order some lab work today, and a thyroid scan as soon as possible."

"What's wrong with me?"

"You have a small mass on your thyroid. It could be nothing, but it's best to check it out. I'll be out of the clinic for the next few weeks, but my colleague, Dr. Jimenez, will follow up on the lab results. If anything shows up on the scan, I'll be in touch ASAP, and we'll go from there."

He ordered the lab tests and thyroid scan via the portable laptop computer in the exam room. He should instruct Maria to add the extra patient visit to his schedule, in order to charge for it, but the numbers game had never mattered to him. As long as Mrs. Peters got the medical attention she needed he'd be satisfied.

Hunter glanced at his watch. He was already a half hour behind schedule and he had only just started his clinic. It would be a long afternoon.

He rushed back into his office to find Sophie sound asleep in her portable bed. She looked so vulnerable, and she deserved better than this, but his sister had insisted he was the only person she trusted with her baby. For the life of him he couldn't understand why.

Maria appeared at his door, handing him another chart. Starting tomorrow, to make life easier for Sophie, he might have to find somewhere closer to Serena Vista to stay. Maybe one of those extended-stay hotels during the week, and then he could go home on the weekends. Didn't nine-month-old babies need to crawl and explore, not sit in a car half the day? If it was just him making the commute, he could handle it, but guilt over his sorely lacking parenting skills had him promising he wouldn't let little Sophie suffer another day.

* * *

The next morning Amanda lifted her gaze from the EKG she'd been analyzing at her desk. She quickly scribbled NSR by the patient's name on the list. Normal sinus rhythm.

Hunter appeared in the office doorway thirty minutes late. Again. Sophie gnawed on his chin as he held her in his arms. "I have an idea," he said.

"You're late," Amanda replied with a no-nonsense glance.

He briskly entered the room and unloaded Sophie's belongings onto his desk. "Sorry. Traffic's a nightmare."

She felt a guilty twinge about being annoyed, but refused to let on.

"Sophie's been a grump all morning, too," he said.

Mandy bristled at his underhanded comment on her mood, but again didn't react.

The sturdy baby sucked on two fingers and looked innocently up at him. "You've been grumpy, haven't you, kid?" He crossed his eyes and made a muffled elephant sound with his lips, which got a giggle out of her. She swatted at his mouth with her slippery fingers. He repeated the goofy process several more times, nibbling her fingertips in between, until she latched onto his chin again and gummed him up something fierce. "I don't have a clue why she likes this, but I've discovered she does, and if it keeps her from crying, my chin is hers."

Amanda fought off a pang of regret for giving him such a hard time. Being a stand-in father had to be a shock for him. But from the looks of things it was becoming second nature, whether he realized it or not.

"You said you had an idea?" she asked.

He plopped Sophie down into her playpen and wiped the drool off his face and jacket. "Music therapy."

"Music what?"

"You know—soothing music to help our patients release stress."

*Our* patients? He'd definitely come on board with her project. "You mean like with meditation?"

"Exactly. We could assign them ten to fifteen minutes of quiet music meditation every morning. It might help bring down their blood pressure."

She thought for a moment. "It wouldn't hurt."

"Great," he said, practically straightening his collar and preening. "I'll put together a list of composers and burn twenty CDs."

"Sounds good."

Sophie glanced up from her playpen and squealed a hello, obviously glad to see Mandy.

"What's up, Soph?" The baby made a series of gurgles, blew some bubbles, and ended by giving Amanda a raspberry.

"I think she wants you to pick her up," Hunter said with a smile.

She didn't take the challenge.

There he was, standing too close again, looking handsome in his white doctor's coat and a piercing silver-blue tie. He'd styled his thick brown hair so that it stood up on the top of his head. It gave him a whimsical appeal—until she glanced into his dark, sexy eyes and suddenly remembered he could also be dangerous. She didn't linger there. She couldn't.

He'd shaved close, except for a small patch just beneath his lower lip—had she noticed that before? She had an unwanted desire to touch it. What would he think if he knew she'd resorted to all but wearing his brand of cologne after he'd moved out to help her feel less lonely?

He inclined his head the slightest bit, studying her, sizing her up, as he'd used to when they were married. He lifted a brow. "Am I making you nervous?" A look of satisfaction stretched across his face.

She brushed him off. When had he become an expert at reading body language? "Not at all." She turned and flipped the desk calendar to today's date—once again all business. "All we have to do today is collect the halter monitor data and analyze it."

She couldn't even glance at him. Instead she pretended to be completely engrossed in the preplanned schedule. "Oh, and don't forget to collect their daily diet journals when you remove the halter monitors."

"Will do." He strolled back to his desk, picked up a piece of paper, returned and handed it to her. "Here's mine. Where's yours? I want to make sure you're getting enough calories."

She pushed his list away. "*You* don't have to report to me."

"The syllabus says *everyone* will participate in the activities. Hand yours over." He motioned with his fingers.

"I… I don't have it."

He raised a playful brow. "Naughty, naughty."

Too young to have hot flashes, she was swiftly burning up. Why was he tormenting her?

"Mandy's not playing fair, Sophie," he teased, picking up the baby, who had now pulled herself to stand in the playpen. Sophie smothered his mouth with her hands. He kept talking, but Amanda couldn't make out one single syllable.

"Okay, okay, I'll start keeping track like everyone else." She had a sudden overwhelming urge to bite the hangnail on her finger, but resisted.

Rather than look at Amanda, he made a clown face for the baby. "There you go." Sophie giggled. "The playing part's kind of fun, but the rest—" He made another face and the baby laughed more.

His frivolity was driving Amanda nuts. She picked up a chart and studied it, determined not to let Hunter lighten her mood. "I'll tell them about the music meditation later, after we go over their EKG results at the group meeting this afternoon."

She tapped her finger on her upper lip. There was no time like the present. "I have a few ideas, too," she said.

"Yeah?" he said over his shoulder, putting Sophie in her jump seat, which he'd just attached to the door frame. The baby automatically started bouncing up and down, making a wide, gummy grin. "See—this is a lifesaver. I can hang her in here and she keeps herself busy for up to an hour sometimes." He rubbed his jaw. "Now, if I could just figure out what to do with her the rest of the time…"

"Hunter." Amanda refused to get sidetracked. "We need to set some ground rules about our professional relationship," she said, noticing how ridiculous she sounded the moment the words left her mouth.

He stood perfectly still, while Sophie ricocheted off the floor as if an atomic particle.

Amanda cleared her throat and tried not to be distracted. "I don't think we should discuss our past at work, or socialize in any way." A flutter of nerves gathered in her stomach, making a tightly bound knot. "And no touching. That should be off-limits, too."

He quirked a brow.

"Anything you'd consider off-limits for your medical assistant, or any female coworker, please do the same for me."

He squinted, took a deep breath as if to say the first thought in his mind, then stopped and regrouped. "Sounds as if you could use some music therapy, too," he grumbled, and stepped around the bouncing baby to leave the room.

Sophie grew fussier as the morning went on, until Hunter couldn't stop her crying.

"Why don't you borrow an otoscope from Peds and check if she's got an ear infection?" Amanda suggested.

"She doesn't feel feverish to me," he said, pressing the back of his hand against her cheek and forehead. "And she's not pulling at her ears. But it's a good idea."

When Hunter whisked Sophie out of the office and headed down the hall for the pediatric clinic, it dawned on her. Sophie was nine months old. She was probably teething. She rooted through the baby bag and came up with a liquid-filled teething ring. After washing her hands and the teething ring with soap and water, she waited for Hunter and Sophie's return.

Soon he reappeared in the doorway, shaking his head. "Not an ear infection."

Sophie whimpered and kicked her legs.

"Teething." She held up the toy to entice Sophie to chew on it, instead of on Hunter's chin and beard stubble.

"Would you like me to take her for a while?"

Hunter nodded gratefully.

When Amanda stepped forward and reached for the child, she noticed the dark circles under Hunter's eyes. She hadn't seen that before—probably because she'd avoided looking at him all morning. Had she put that on the no-no list? No eye contact? Maybe she'd add it, because as she recalled, his haunting dark eyes could work better than Svengali's when it came to getting his way.

The poor guy had probably been up all night with a fussy baby. She regretted chiding him for being late again. His world had been turned sideways, having Sophie thrust on him right before he'd been hoodwinked into mentoring the Mending Hearts Club project. Truth was, she felt kind of sorry for him, and she wanted to make amends…to both of them. She also felt a major reversal coming on. For crying out loud, it had only taken two days.

"You know, Hunter, my house is only five minutes away. Why don't you and Sophie go there and take a nap during lunch? It might do you both good." That doesn't qualify as socializing, does it? So what if the guy would have full access to where she lived? She wouldn't be there. Was it too late to take back the offer?

He hesitated, making a thin line with his lips. "I couldn't do that."

Okay, good. She could back out now. He was right. He couldn't and shouldn't do that. "No. Really. You should." Had she lost control of her mouth?

"I'd be breaking one of your rules," he teased.

Underneath her professional facade, she was a person, a person with a heart. The guy needed to catch a break and she could give it to him. She'd do the same for any of her coworkers.

"This is an exception. You both look worn-out, and I can't afford for you to get so run-down that you get sick."

"Since you put it that way," he said, fighting off a smirk, "I'll take you up on the offer."

Amanda fished through her purse and found her keys. She dangled them before him. "Turn left out of the driveway, go to the second light and turn right. I'm the third condo from the corner. Ground level. One-one-seven."

"Thanks," he said, snatching the keys from her hand—but not before he'd held her fingers for a moment. Staring deeply into her eyes, he said, "Sorry. I'm not supposed to do that, am I?" He caught her off guard with his charming smile and a quick wink. "You know me. I like breaking rules."

That was precisely what she was afraid of.

# CHAPTER THREE

HUNTER dug into his pocket with a damp palm for the house keys Mandy had given him. How would it feel to invade her privacy after being away all these years?

The door opened to a bright living room, much as he'd expected, and a house that smelled of flowers and grilled vegetables. Mandy had always been a healthy eater.

One long lime-green divan covered with flashy throw pillows and two loudly patterned chairs were an obvious change in her style. Candles were everywhere, almost like a shrine, and it made him worry she spent too much time alone…in the dark. Dried flower arrangements and picture frames were perched on bookcases and tables. Not one photograph was from their time together. Strangely, it made him feel forgotten.

He recognized an oil painting she'd bought when they were married, one they'd chosen together, and remembered how much he'd liked the abstract style after she'd convinced him to open up his artistic tastes.

A family shot taken of Mandy and her parents stood out. Her dutiful daughter role. To the common eye no one would notice her smile was ever so slightly strained. But he knew better. They'd never had any faith in Mandy, and it used to cut to her core. He, on the other hand, had encouraged her to go after her dreams…until she'd admitted to him *everything* she desired from life and their marriage. But that story had ended, and maybe it was best not to open the book again.

Hunter had resisted the breakup, preferring things to go on as they always had, but Mandy had dug in her heels and insisted on a divorce due to irreconcilable differences. He still scratched his head at her change of heart about having a baby. After their problem had been naturally resolved when she'd got her period, he'd expected her to join him with a *Whew, that was a close call* attitude and drop it. But she'd changed. Her career and marriage had no longer been enough. She'd given him no choice.

Hunter glanced at Sophie, asleep in her portable car seat. Though caring for her was only temporary, he feared the baby was already being neglected because of his job. He'd had to tote her everywhere, to depend on the kindness of others to see to her while he worked, then pack her up and confine her in the car for more travel. Which she hated. How could a child grow and be healthy under such circumstances? And what more proof did he need about mixing families with demanding careers? He and Jade had paid a big price for their parents' successes, and he was damned if he'd make his children suffer, too. Nope. No babies for him.

A sturdy oak dining table sat before an entire wall of sliding glass doors that overlooked a covered patio. Pushing aside a stack of papers, he put the car seat in the middle of the table. Why, he wondered, did she have such a large table for one person? He didn't need to think for long. Being an only child had always been lonely for Mandy. Even now she obviously still dreamed of filling her table and home with a family. A big family.

He glanced outside and spotted healthy potted plants. Were

they real? He shook his head remorsefully at the lack of faith he'd shown in Mandy years before. Just like her parents.

Hunter set up the portable baby bed in a snug corner, and gingerly lifted Sophie from her car seat—hoping with all his might he wouldn't wake her up. She fussed the slightest bit. *Please, no.* He worried she'd start crying again, but she didn't. Instead she snuggled down into her soft blanket and fell deeper into her dreams.

He heaved a sigh of relief.

At the beginning of a long hall, he found a bedroom on the right, abutting the living room. It was Mandy's. He inhaled her unmistakable scent. Was it rosemary she'd once said had been added to lavender? A sudden heady feeling followed a memory of having watched her apply lotion to her legs with long strokes after a shower.

Even if this was the only bed in the house, no way could he lie on it. He'd use the sofa. Why torture himself with memories of stretching side by side, flesh to flesh with his wife? He made a proprietorial survey for any telltale signs of another man. Negative.

A sly smile extended across his lips.

Closing the door, he walked farther down the hall toward the bathroom at the end. What the hell was that smell? It was pungent and foul, as if her plumbing might be backed up. No wonder she had potpourri all over the place. He closed the guest bathroom and the laundry room doors, then headed for the one remaining bedroom on the other side of the hall.

After a quick look around, he took off his jacket and flopped onto the mattress covered with a flowery spread. He didn't give a damn that it was another girly room as long as he could get some sleep.

Just as he was about to doze off, a soft thud next to his head made his lids fly open. He stared into a pair of devious amber-colored eyes. He'd been stalked, and now he knew what that damn smell was.

Cat box.

By three o'clock there was still no sign of Hunter. Amanda didn't have the heart to call home and wake him up. It was obvious Hunter and Sophie both needed their rest.

All she'd been doing was removing halter monitors and collecting food journals with each patient's appointment. She could take the remaining EKGs and diet journals home to analyze if she didn't finish them all here. Then she'd enter the data into her home computer after her shift in the Urgent Care clinic that night.

At a quarter to five, just as she was packing up, Hunter appeared in the office, looking rested but disheveled. "Mandy, I'm so sorry. If Sophie hadn't soaked her diaper we'd still be asleep."

"I was beginning to wonder…" A slight smile twitched at the edges of her mouth. He looked so…slept-in.

"How can I make it up to you? Do you want me to stay late?"

How like him to show up ready to work rather than call and see if he could get out of coming back, she thought briefly. "No. Go home, get a good night's rest, and show up on time tomorrow. We'll be running the stress tests and dividing everyone into exercise groups."

"Sounds like a plan. I'll see you tomorrow, then." He tossed her the keys.

She nodded, already preoccupied with the last EKG, pretending to be distracted. "See ya."

He turned to leave. "Nice condo, by the way."

For some silly reason, the compliment made her happy. "Thanks."

"Should have told me about the cat, though."

She fought back that tickly smile again, eventually giving in and grinning at the desk.

That evening, Amanda hadn't been home more than fifteen minutes when someone knocked on her door. There stood Hunter, carrying Sophie in her car seat. The baby happily gnawed away at her teething ring, but made a quick kick and squeal when she noticed Amanda.

"What are you doing here?"

"Two diesel trucks jackknifed on the freeway and caught on fire. All lanes are shut down until further notice, and the detour will take a good two hours."

"Then you'll just have to stay here." What in the world had she just said?

"You wouldn't mind?"

Of course she would! "Not at all. You've already found the guest room. You and Sophie can set up in there."

"What about all those ground rules you laid down?"

She sighed with indecision. Ah, hell. "They don't apply in an emergency."

He carried all the baby items he could hold through the door. "I owe you. I couldn't stand the thought of sitting in traffic another minute."

Hunter's eyes came to rest on her legs. She'd just gotten ready to take a quick run before her shift, and had on nothing more than flimsy jogging shorts and a midriff-length T-shirt. Her cheeks burned with heat by the time Hunter glanced back up into her eyes.

"Am I interrupting something?" he said. "Besides your entire life, I mean?"

He pointedly tried not to check her legs out again, but her cheeks flamed hotter. She palmed her face with a cool hand, then pretended to find her carotid artery and time her pulse.

"Going for a run. Make yourself at home," she said over her shoulder, and she bolted out the door.

Hunter stood and stared until she was halfway down the block. She was a natural runner, her arms relaxed at her sides, shoulders straight. He smiled at her long, smooth strides. The rump shot was fantastic, too.

The short-furred gray tabby came down the hall to take a peek. He didn't know if the cat was allowed outside or not, so he held him back with his foot and regretfully closed the door.

Sophie fussed, as if to say, *Well? Are we staying or not?*

Great. Now he was interpreting baby thoughts. Well, that was better than the wicked ones running around his mind right then.

He cleared his throat. "Okay. Okay. Give me a second, will you, Sophie?"

The baby gave him a juicy raspberry.

"Back at ya, kid."

He had to be nuts to have accepted Mandy's invitation. It meant spending the evening in each other's company, and that would be easy on neither of them. Being around her would dredge up old feelings, and, frankly, he'd used most of his sentimental reserves caring for Sophie.

As if he needed more convincing, he cracked open the door for one last look at Mandy jogging away. Yeah, that rump shot was spectacular.

* * *

"You're working at Urgent Care tonight?" Hunter had made himself at home, removed his jacket and, because of the mid-summer heat, stripped down to his undershirt. If he were at home, he would have had on shorts, and most likely wouldn't be wearing a shirt at all.

Mandy, on the other hand, had showered and changed back into work clothes.

"Uh-huh. I had to take a leave of absence to work on the heart project, but I moonlight a couple of shifts a week." She nibbled on a protein bar. "The grant I got for the study allows for a small stipend, but it doesn't cover enough of my expenses. And even though Mercy Hospital is donating the Serena Vista Clinic office space, special equipment and classrooms, I still need money to live on."

"Who's paying me?"

"Mercy Hospital. Like always."

"Why aren't they paying *you*…like always?"

"Because I'm not seeing patients as a nurse practitioner."

"That doesn't seem fair. I'm not seeing patients anymore, either."

"Sure you are. The Mending Hearts Club patients. Anyway, it's my study, and I'm happy to do it, so I'm not going to sweat the small stuff."

"The small stuff? Like your life and livelihood?" She'd always had a "work is life" attitude, but this was ridiculous.

She took another bite from the bar. "It's not so bad. Help yourself to any food." She grabbed a banana. "I should be home around eleven."

Once again she bolted out the door, leaving Hunter angry about the injustice of the hospital system, worried that the protein bar would be her only dinner, and relieved he wouldn't have to spend the entire evening with her. And if that wasn't a crazy enough mix of concerns, one other feeling edged its way into his mind—disappointment.

Marian Jamison, a longtime friend and fellow NP, listened attentively as Amanda explained the recent crazy change of circumstances and twist of fate in her life. Marian lifted a single blond brow when Amanda mentioned Hunter was back at her house this very minute and would be spending the night.

"Is he still as hot as he used to be?" Marian's playful green gaze twinkled with mischief.

Amanda took a deep breath and rolled her eyes. "That's beside the point, Marian. He's juggling his niece and commuting, and trying to be useful with the patients, and I want this heart study to be a success more than anything."

"Apparently. Or you wouldn't have Hunter sleeping over."

"It's not like that, and you know it." But the thought of Hunter sleeping under the same roof sent a tickle down her spine, and she curled her toes to try to stop the feeling.

If only she could have encouraged him to find a hotel without feeling like a witch.

Before Marian could utter another smart remark, Amanda shook her head and strode to the next patient exam room. She tapped on the door and entered. A grizzled-haired man with tented brows and apprehensive eyes nodded her a greeting. She suspected he was in pain. She introduced herself and offered her hand.

He winced when he moved his arm away from his body to shake.

"What brought you to Urgent Care, Mr. Salcedo?"

"I've had a fever for a couple of days. Thought I was coming down with the flu, you know. I ache all over and I'm very tired."

She glanced at the computer notes left by the medical assistant who had checked his vitals. Elevated b/p and temp.

"Now I have terrible pain around my ribs." Tension creased the corners of his eyes.

"On both sides?"

"Just on this side." He gingerly touched his right side above the waist.

"Did you fall or bump into anything lately?"

The simple act of shaking his head caused him to wince again.

"Any history of kidney stones?"

Another head shake.

"Let's have a look." There was no evidence of bruising. "What does the pain feel like?"

"Like burning and aching. It's nonstop."

"Just on the one side?"

He nodded.

She put on gloves and checked the skin closely for any signs of early outbreak. "Did you have chicken pox as a child?"

He nodded again.

"Ever hear of shingles?"

His eyes widened. "Yes."

Sophie popped into Amanda's mind. Had she had all of her immunizations? Especially the varicella zoster shot? Just in case, she'd be sure to change her clothes and wash her hands before going near Sophie tonight, if she was still awake. *Focus.* She chided herself for letting her mind wander to Hunter and his niece. Again.

"I see the beginning of a couple of blisters toward your spine. It looks like classic shingles, Mr. Salcedo. I'm going to have the doctor prescribe an antiviral medicine and something for the pain. Start taking both right away. Do not scratch the blisters as they appear or you'll spread them around. And wash your hands anytime you come in contact with them." She flipped the call light for a medical assistant before sitting at the computer to type her assessment and findings. "I'll have the nurse explain how to apply damp dressings for comfort, and a special lotion to help dry up the breakout. And avoid anyone who hasn't had chicken pox yet as long as you're breaking out. You could infect them."

The man nodded after each instruction, his anxious expression already smoothing out from knowing help was on its way.

"The breakout could last for several weeks, and sometimes the pain lingers. Come back and see us immediately if you develop facial or eye pain, or blisters around the ears or eyes."

His brows drew together again.

"Just make sure you wash your hands if you touch the blisters," she reiterated. "I'll go have the doctor write a prescription for you." She finished her computer entry just as the MA arrived. As she left the room, she said, "Mr. Salcedo needs shingles education. Thanks."

Once back at the shared desk, having hand-delivered the prescription to Mr. Salcedo, Amanda found Marian—who was ready with her next batch of questions.

"So what could be the worst that could happen if you let Hunter stay at your house for as long as he has his niece?"

"A month? Are you nuts?"

Marian scratched her chin before adding, "You said yourself that you are *so over him*. Remember?"

*Maybe I lied.* Amanda tossed her gaze across the room rather than make eye contact with her friend.

"You're civilized adults, right?" Marian said. "And this is the twenty-first century." She fiddled with her stethoscope while waiting for an answer.

"What's the worst that could happen?" Amanda tapped her foot and thought for a moment before she went to her next patient. Then she mumbled, "I'd get used to having him around again."

Amanda tried to be as quiet as possible when she returned home at 11:30 p.m., but she found Hunter in the dark living room, watching the news. He sat on the couch with his bare feet resting on the coffee table. The silhouette of his broad shoulders knocked her off-kilter. His hair looked mussed and spiky, and he had one muscular arm propped behind his head.

He must have dozed off, because he didn't respond to her arrival. She walked quietly to the dining table and put her purse on a chair.

At this angle, she had to smile. Jinx, her cat, was curled up on his lap.

Hunter's head shot up.

"Hey," she said softly.

"Hey. Must have fallen asleep."

"How's Sophie doing?"

"Great. After I fed and bathed her she went right to sleep." He gently lifted Jinx and plopped him on the floor.

"Maybe that new tooth has broken through," she said.

"Last time I tried to check, she practically bit off my finger."

Despite being on her guard, Amanda caught herself chuckling. She stretched to avoid his gaze. Jinx rubbed against her leg and she bent to scratch his ears, grateful for the distraction.

"Anything exciting happen tonight?" he asked.

"I had to remove a cockroach from an old guy's ear."

"No kidding? Can't say I've ever done that."

He stood, and Amanda's heart dropped to her stomach at the

sight. He was wearing only black boxers. "You look tired," he said, using the remote to mute the TV.

She diverted her gaze before he could notice, but she'd already taken inventory of his flat stomach and muscled chest. "I'm fine." She backed away.

He glanced at himself and gave her a knowing look. "It's not like you've never seen me like this before."

Her accusing stare didn't seem to bother him in the least.

"I've been thinking," he said, scratching his head and walking closer.

Aware of a warm blush, she backed away more at the old and familiar phrase. "Really?" She noticed the scent of lingering cologne and fought off any further reaction.

"I was planning on renting a room at the local extended-stay hotel for the duration of the class, but if I stayed here instead I could pay *you*. Then it would seem more like a home for Sophie during the week, and you wouldn't have to work those extra shifts…"

"I like keeping my hand in patient care." *And no way could she live with him.*

"Sure. But at what expense to you physically? You're not an iron woman. You've gotten so thin a good breeze could blow you over." He walked closer, the TV light dappling his face in shadows.

Taking offense, she swallowed around a dry knot. "Let me handle things, Hunter. I had everything planned before you ever stepped in. If you need to rent a room at a hotel, do it."

"I'm just trying to help, Mandy."

*Right. Help drive me crazy.*

"Thanks, but Sophie should be your only concern." She started to walk down the hall. "Good night."

Hunter hurtled over the back of the couch and caught up

with her. He grabbed her wrist and pulled her back. "I don't understand why you won't let me help you. We can help each other, Mandy."

Before she could ask, he let go of her arm, but their gazes remained locked in place. She knew he wouldn't back down. Her arm tingled where he'd touched her, and those dark eyes delved into hers, making it hard to focus on any particular thought.

He felt too close. She needed to get away.

"You don't honestly think we could live together as if nothing had ever happened, do you?" she asked.

"No. But we could take it one day at a time and see how things go. And we could help each other out of a tough situation." He looked so damn earnest she had to look away. "Truth is, I could use your help with Sophie, too."

"I don't want your money, and, sorry, but Sophie is your responsibility. Not mine."

"You're refusing a perfectly sane offer to make both our lives less complicated."

"It would only make things *more* complicated, and you know it."

"I'll stay out of your hair, Mandy. I promise. And Sophie *will* be my responsibility. I'm just trying to help you out a little. It seems to me you could use a break."

She glared at him, but quickly softened when she saw how sincere he looked.

"I'll think about it," she said, and slipped down the hall to her room.

Just as she reached for the doorknob, he said, "So, how'd you do it?"

"Do what?"

"Get that cockroach out?"

"I took the patient into a dark closet and shone a flashlight in his ear. The sucker practically jumped into my gloves."

She closed the bedroom door on Hunter's warm rumble of laughter, and a tiny voice in the dark recesses of her mind suddenly wondered what would be so bad about having him around.

A rude, blaring buzz shocked Amanda out of a deep sleep. It gathered her up from a peaceful dream and threw her smack into the middle of reality, sunlight and morning. She'd stayed up until after one, entering patient data into her computer.

She groped and felt around like a child in the dark. Once she'd turned off the damn buzzer, she stretched and sat up, tested her feet on the floor, and slid them into her favorite fuzzy slippers. A monumentally huge yawn occupied the next several seconds.

Three, two, one—blastoff. On autopilot, she launched herself toward the bedroom door and down the hall, heading for the kitchen. Her mission: to plug in the coffeepot of decaffeinated coffee before she showered.

Slap-slide, slap-slide. Eyes half-closed, she shuffled across the living room and toward the kitchen…into a completely dressed Hunter.

"Aaaah! What are you doing here?" Her eyes stretched wide open.

"Having a cup of decaf, since that's all you've got. Good morning." He nodded, lifting the cup. "Say hi, Sophie."

The baby hung in her jump seat from the pantry door frame, and bounced excitedly up and down.

Amanda couldn't help noticing an amused look on Hunter's freshly shaven face as his eyes lazily glided over her body and came to rest below her chin. Turnabout was fair play. She'd seen him in his underwear; now he was seeing her in hers.

"Uh…hi. Need to put some clothes on…"

She spun around and zipped back to her room as fast as her fuzzy slippers allowed, "Jeez," being her only outburst.

"I take it back," he called out. "You're not as skinny as I'd thought."

During the night, she'd tossed and turned about whether or not to take Hunter up on his offer. Sure, the extra money would help her out, but that wasn't a good enough reason to subject herself to the torment of having Hunter *and* a baby around all the time. The constant reminder of the very thing she'd wanted but would never have had with Hunter would be more than she could bear.

In the end, after more tossing and turning, it had been Jade and her circumstances that had turned the tide of Amanda's thoughts. What if things had been reversed and Amanda had been the one with a baby? The one who needed to be hospitalized? If she were a mother and for some awful reason couldn't take care of her baby, wouldn't she appreciate someone stepping up to help out? Yes, being around Sophie and Hunter would be torture, but Jade had been a good friend throughout Amanda's marriage, and sometimes doing the right thing was more important than avoiding personal conflict.

So she'd decided to let Hunter and Sophie stay with her throughout the Mending Hearts Club class, at least for as long as Jade was hospitalized, and had planned to tell him this morning. Suddenly her biggest concern was not how to break the news, but how to face him for the rest of the day without cringing or blushing.

# CHAPTER FOUR

THE next morning, after the group had checked in, Amanda lectured on the day's topic of "Blood Pressure and General Well-Being" and handed out several heart-health-related articles for the participants to read. Then she counseled everyone individually, before sending them along for their treadmill stress tests.

She glanced at the diet journal of her first student.

"Mr. Mancuso, it says here you ate dinner out at a steak house last night?"

The portly man nodded, his arms crossed. "I'm not giving up meat."

She measured his reply and thought how best to broach the topic. "You don't have to give up red meat entirely. Though I do advocate that, I understand how many people love their steak." She remembered the last time a giant hamburger had absconded with her good sense. "Portion size is the key."

She glanced into flat, unwavering eyes.

"If you immediately cut the restaurant steak serving in half, you'll have the other half to take home and enjoy another day. And to help satisfy your appetite, be sure to order a salad with your meal. Pick a low-fat dressing and ask for it on the side."

Spotting a glimmer of interest, she fanned the flame. "Mr. Mancuso, you and I both know you're here because your doctor is worried about you. And I bet if I asked your wife she'd admit to being worried about you, too."

He uncrossed his arms.

"Our goal is to give you a long life, and it only takes a few adjustments to help your health along. Can you work with me here?"

Almost imperceptibly, his face softened. She smiled to coax him along. "It's all about eating slowly, savoring the taste, and having smaller portions."

He scratched his head. "So, what's my daily protein serving size again?"

She beamed. "Four to six ounces—the size of the palm of your hand. If you have a salad for lunch, then you can splurge with an eight-ounce steak."

Now he smiled.

"But you can only do that once a week. The rest of the time you've got to eat chicken or fish."

He scratched his balding head. "I guess I can live with that."

"And live a lot longer, too!" She shook his hand.

The moment he left the office, her mind went back to Hunter and Sophie. Amanda had done an amazing job of avoiding Hunter all morning by lecturing on blood pressure, and saturated and trans fats, and their role in heart disease. Hunter had been relegated to running the stress tests in the clinic cardiology department.

Thankfully, since that morning at home, she hadn't had to look into his eyes and see what could only be interpreted as desire when he'd seen her in her undergarments. She had to be nuts, deciding to let him stay with her for the duration of the class, but she'd made up her mind to do it for both Jade and Sophie's sakes. And in light of her decision, one thing was for sure: from now on she'd only wear old gray sweats around the house, regardless of the temperature.

Too bad her conscience wouldn't allow her to send them to the extended-stay hotel—life would be so much easier. But she couldn't bring herself to do that.

Amanda worried about Jade that the darkness that had overtaken her life would consume her without a daily dose of her little ball of sunlight. And what better way to remind Jade of unconditional love than Sophie's smile? But Jade was in the hospital and would be treated for her illness, and the reward for dealing with her depression would be coming home to her daughter.

She wondered if Hunter was able to be in touch with Jade yet, and how she was doing. The baby needed stability while her mother got treated for depression, and she didn't deserve to keep being shuffled from one place to another. Not to mention a long commute. Which was all the more reason to invite them to stay with her.

The fact that Hunter had offered to help out financially was an unexpected and not totally unwelcome bonus—and so like him. All things considered, it seemed like a win-win situation. And accepting money from him would help keep their relationship on a strictly business level.

Who said she couldn't change?

But since Hunter had appeared in her life again, each moment spent too close to him threatened to reopen the old wound. She'd often likened her emotional healing process from the divorce to the surgical method of healing by granulation. Slowly the wound filled in with soft, sensitive tissue but bled easily. Over time the same tissue toughened up and made a cicatrix. But her protective scar wasn't quite complete, and she feared living with Hunter would be like running with scissors toward a runaway train.

She sighed. Never in her life did she want to experience that kind of pain again. But for Sophie and Jade she'd take the chance....

Amanda glanced up in time to see Hunter and Sophie enter the office. Her throat tensed and went dry at the sight of them.

She and Hunter nodded a greeting, then both quickly looked away—though not before he seemed to sense that she'd been thinking about them. Her warm cheeks must have given her away.

Sophie looked on the verge of falling asleep. Making great strides on the parenting learning curve, Hunter quickly took his cue to throw a bottle together for the baby and put her down for a nap.

In the past, Amanda would have lectured him on the bad effect of formula and milk on baby teeth. Or made sure he knew about the importance of holding the baby when feeding her. Today she didn't have the heart. Instead, she kept busy and avoided him by dividing the class into two exercise groups for tomorrow's first physical training event.

"Jack Howling took the stress test all the way to the top," Hunter said from his desk, booting up his laptop. "I can only hope to be as fit at fifty."

"That's great." Amanda gave an uninspired reply and a nod of the head.

Hunter shuffled through his drawer for a moment, produced what he was looking for—an iPod with headphones—then sidled up to her desk and sat on the edge.

"Here. You should listen to this before I burn off copies for everyone."

He was too close. Again. And wearing the same tie he'd worn yesterday. The poor guy needed to make a trip home for more supplies and a wardrobe for both he and Sophie.

She almost jerked when he gently touched each of her ears by inserting first one earpiece and then the other. Only separated by the length of the cords from the device he held, she could barely stand it. She watched him swallow. Being near enough to notice a small nick on his throat where he'd had to use her pink disposable razor to shave almost made her dizzy.

Focusing back in, she heard the music that was at first soothing. But as it went along, it built and grew livelier, until finally a booming bass made her heartbeat speed up.

Amanda quickly pulled the plugs from her ears. "Techno?"

"That's to pump them up and energize them for the day."

She placed the earphones in his palms and said, "I thought we were going for meditation and relaxation?"

"And the first portion does that. But we don't want to put them to sleep, either. We need to rev them up and get them started. Especially since the Diet Journal Queen says they can only have decaf."

She rolled her eyes and pushed her chair back. "We're not going to get into role-playing here, are we? Where you're the nice parent and I'm the mean parent? I'm doing the no-caffeine thing for their own good."

"A little java jolt once in a while isn't going to hurt anyone."

*It could hurt me.*

Thankfully, Hunter had touched on her inner witch, and turned her previously sympathetic thoughts into angry ones. They'd always been great sparring partners when they didn't see eye to eye.

Fighting the flare of temper, she refused to make the mistake of glancing into his dark and fathomless eyes. That had always gotten her into trouble. She swallowed…and backed down from his challenge. She wouldn't let Hunter entice her into old routines, when they'd used to end their notorious fighting with passion in the bedroom.

"Okay. Fine with me." She tossed her hair and, seemingly placated, went about her business. Would he put two and two together?

After a long silence, she said, "I'm going to take my lunch break now," and marched toward the door, hoping not to trip over her strange new self-restraint. But an important thought occurred to her. "Oh, and I've decided you and Sophie are welcome to stay with me. You don't have to pay me, but if you insist just come up with a reasonable amount."

Before she could make it out the door, he grabbed her arm and spun her around. Surprised, she stared into his eyes.

He gave her a loaded, teasing smile. "Maybe we could barter services for lodging?"

The old single-minded Hunter had reared his sexy head. She wasn't about to fall for that too-familiar charm. Calling his bluff, she said, "Five hundred a week. No perks." She removed her arm from his grasp and slipped out the door without looking back.

"Thanks," he called after her. "What's for dinner?"

That evening, Hunter left Sophie with Amanda while he drove home for more baby supplies and clothes.

While Amanda sat stiffly, Sophie sat contentedly on her lap. She tried not to breathe in her baby freshness or study her pudgy perfection. The tiny girl tugged at her heartstrings, but Amanda couldn't indulge herself. It's only temporary, she reminded herself. There's no point in getting attached. Her gaze darted around the room rather than watch the baby for one more moment. Now she understood how Hunter felt. *What the heck should I do with her?*

Her instinct told her to smother her with kisses and fuss over her, to love her up and make silly noises and play peek-a-boo, but she couldn't allow herself to do that. Sophie wasn't hers. Neither was Hunter.

Just that morning she'd noticed how much the baby enjoyed jumping. At a loss for what to do, she held her at a distance, pulled her up by the waist, and let her bounce on her thighs. Soon, all Sophie needed to hold on to were Amanda's fingers. When Sophie locked her knees, her plump little legs felt strong and ready to support her.

As a nursing experiment, Amanda placed her on the floor beside the coffee table to let her anchor herself and stand. She knew at this age some babies were strong enough to hold themselves up and balance all by themselves. After a few bounces, amazingly, Sophie stood still for one full moment without the help of anything, before she plopped down on her padded bottom and crawled away.

Amanda's heart burst for Jade. She'd missed a key moment in her daughter's development. She shook her head. No, she hadn't. Jade would be home soon enough, and she would see it for herself *for the first time*. All Amanda had to do was keep her mouth shut.

"Come on, let's give you a bath," she said, and she swooped Sophie up and headed for the guest bathroom.

A pleasant, prurient memory of Mandy standing before him that morning in nothing but French-cut panties and a spaghetti-strapped undershirt looped over and over in Hunter's mind while he drove home. Nothing had been left to his imagination. He'd especially liked the fresh-out-of-bed hair. It had made him want to smooth it into place…made him want to do a few other things, too.

He admitted to watching each step when she had shuffled quickly back down the hall. Derrieres that great were rare. Nature's beauty should be admired, he'd always said, and that belief was as firm as Mandy's backside.

So why did he feel compelled to stick around his house to copy some of the CDs for the class instead of rushing back to

Mandy's? Because living with Mandy would be unadulterated torture. And, since he was in stalling mode, he decided to stop at the market on the way back to get some of the things *he* liked to eat. If they were going to be living together, he might as well enjoy it.

Hunter made a point to time his dinner with Mandy's that night. As he recalled, she preferred to eat late. After he'd gotten home and unpacked, he heard her puttering around in the kitchen and sprang into action.

Mandy looked over her shoulder and shot him an embarrassed smile when he entered the room.

"Hey." He nodded a greeting. He suspected she was thinking about their morning encounter. He didn't want her to know he was, too, though he definitely still was.

"Hey, Hunt." She sounded less than enthusiastic.

He paused at the familiar nickname before reaching into the freezer to pull out the "meat loaf and taters" ready meal he'd just bought.

"Thanks for putting Sophie to bed."

"No problem."

Seeing that she had a glass of wine going, he opened the refrigerator and retrieved a beer—another of his purchases. He unscrewed the lid and took a long draw from the bottle, waiting for conversation to sprout.

Mandy washed, dried and scattered wads of romaine lettuce into a large bowl, then glanced over her shoulder. "Want to eat together?"

"Sure. Why not?" he said, suppressing his pleasure.

She lifted her wine, sipped and crinkled her nose with a sweet smile. "Listen, I've got oodles of lettuce here—would you like a salad with your meat loaf meal?"

The last time he'd heard the word "oodles" was when they were married. It was one of her favorite expressions. *I've got oodles of time. Want to make love?* A quick melancholic pang took him by surprise. Ever since seeing her half-naked, his mind had been on one thing.

"Don't mind if I do. Good thing I'm not drinking wine. I'm not sure which would work with this." He held up the frozen food box for her scrutiny. "Red or white?"

She smiled again. "Beer it is."

Two smiles in a row—he was on a roll.

Hunter glanced at the microwave heating instructions as he popped the container inside. He squinted at the numbers on the oven and poked a few buttons, then leaned against the counter and folded his arms while his dinner cooked.

"I noticed in the diet portion of the syllabus that you don't allow alcohol for the participants, but it's a known fact that a glass of wine a day can be good for your heart."

"That's true, but I don't want to encourage anyone with a drinking problem to drink."

"Didn't you screen every participant?"

"Yes, but sometimes people don't admit to overdrinking."

"Hmm. What are you going to tell the class when they see your diet journal?"

"If you're trying to bother me, I'm not going to let you. No mushrooms for you, right?" she asked.

Mandy was still great at changing topics she didn't want to discuss. "Right." At least she hadn't forgotten about his aversion to mushrooms. He wondered if she'd be surprised that he still remembered the recipe for her special salad dressing.

Mandy reached for a plastic container inside the refrigerator. No doubt it was the secret salad sauce, which automatically made his mouth water. He watched her bend over as he tugged on his beer, noticing she'd traded in yesterday's jogging shorts for sweatpants. He could still make out the outline of her French-cut panties, and tried not to feel like a lowlife for noticing. But he couldn't quite tear his eyes away.

She closed the fridge and slipped a crusty bread roll into the toaster oven to heat. She caught his gaze. He scratched his neck and pretended he'd been looking at the wall calendar.

The microwave beeper dinged. His *manly* meal was done.

Mandy snatched the bread from the toaster oven and headed for the table.

Hunter carried her wine over and offered to top it up. She shook her head, but mouthed thanks.

"Everything in moderation, eh?" Now they'd sat together, he felt compelled to start a regular conversation. "Is the Serena Vista Urgent Care much different from Mercy's ER?"

"Oh, the sun and the moon." She forked a large bite of salad into her mouth and chewed.

"You don't get emergencies there, do you?"

"Sure we do. But the real traumas go to the local hospital instead of our clinic. One time this guy gave me a finger," she said.

He nodded. "What is it with people these days? So rude." He took another swig of beer.

She smiled, and it pleased him, though it stopped his train of thought for a second.

"No." She grinned. "He literally tried to hand me his finger."

"Hmm." He chewed on a potato. His head shot up when her comment sank in. "You're serious."

"Yeah. He'd sliced it off at work. Poor guy. If he'd gone straight to the hospital ER, they may have been able to save it. What a mess. There was blood all over the place. I had him drop it into saline and sent for our on-call surgeon, who was working over at the local ER."

Hunter cut a slice of meat loaf, studied it and made a face before placing it into his mouth. Only half a glass of wine and Mandy had really lightened up. Maybe it was his charming personality? The lack of tension between them was refreshing, even if the conversation was unappetizing.

"Sorry. Didn't mean to gross you out," she said, taking a big bite of salad and chomping down.

"Nah. You know nothing much bothers me. I could tell you stories from my residency that would turn your stomach."

"I know. And you used to," she said, after another large bite. "All the time." He remembered Mandy didn't mind talking with her mouth full. "You know, there's probably two days' worth of salt allotment in that single frozen meal." She pointed with her fork toward his microwave-safe plate, making an obvious topic segue.

He glanced at the huge bite he was about to shove in his mouth and suddenly, between the finger story and the salt issue, no longer felt hungry.

They continued the meal in silence, while he picked at his salad and some bread. Even her delicious poppy seed dressing hadn't brought his appetite back.

When they'd finished eating, the two of them worked like a team, shoulder to shoulder, washing and drying the dishes. It was a routine they'd practiced to perfection during their marriage and easily slipped back into. The silence agonized Hunter, but for the life of him he couldn't think of a single thing to say. It forced him to focus on the ticking of the clock on the wall and the warm, damp scent of lemon soap in the sink…and the nearness of Mandy.

This would have to stop. Maybe living with Mandy wasn't such a good idea after all. He stepped away to finish drying the salad bowls.

She placed the last dish in the cupboard and moseyed into the living room, where she plopped down to read from a stack of medical journals. Hunter was left to fold and hang the damp dish towel.

"Don't forget to record your dinner in your journal," he said, feeling bereft of all social skills and like a complete idiot.

"Oh. Right. Thanks for the reminder." She didn't even glance up.

He scratched his chin and searched his mind for any thread of pithy conversation. *Nada.* The scene was turning into agony.

He'd brought his laptop to her house and planned to copy the rest of the music CDs tonight. He'd quickly learned that, once asleep, Sophie would doze through anything, and since it would be agony to stay in the same room as Mandy without watching her every move, he decided to work in his bedroom.

He started for the hall, but stopped abruptly to make one last attempt at witty repartee.

"Do you want me to make the decaf tomorrow? Or should I wait for the padding of your large fuzzy slippers?"

Hunter glanced over his shoulder, waiting for Mandy's response, and watched her squirm. Her big blues opened wide over the medical journal. She knew exactly what he was thinking. A subtle, pleased twitch formed at the corners of his mouth. She made a stealthy but noticeable reach and threw a small couch pillow at him.

He caught it deftly.

"You can make it, smart-ass, since you seem to get up before I do," she said with unwavering eyes.

"Blame Sophie for that." He held up the pillow. "Now I get why they call these things throw pillows," he said, before he flung it at her like a Frisbee. She dodged, but it lightly pinged the top of her head. She squealed, and he hit the hall as if making a final sprint for the finishing line.

A quick flashback from the past had him in the middle of a wild chase through their old house, with Mandy hot on his trail. She'd caught him and jumped onto his back, laughing and kicking, and like a stallion he'd carried her piggyback-style to their bed, where he'd thrown her onto the mattress and joined her, pouncing on top.

A flurry of sexual images snapped through his mind until he put a stop to them. Standing outside his bedroom door, he listened for any promising sound coming from the living room—a guy could always hope—but he didn't hear a single creak.

Things weren't the same and never would be.

So much for the past and its misleading memories, he thought as he closed the door.

Amanda took a deep breath and tried to slow down her heart. She'd let her guard down and slipped into old familiar habits with Hunter. It had seemed so easy. Yes, she had tried to entice him into a pillow fight—they'd used to have them frequently. He'd followed her lead and fired back. But when it had been her turn to respond, something had held her back. Memories? Nah.

Heart palpitations.

Twice during dinner she'd felt a spurt of them. She knew the warning signs: first the heart fluttered off and on, slipping into an unsteady rhythm, then the episodes would grow closer, until they linked together and became a marathon run of palpitations. It had only happened twice in the last year, and there had never been anything obvious that had set it off, but since her diagnosis, she'd hoped the medicine she'd been taking would keep the unstable beats at bay.

When Amanda had finally been diagnosed with Wolff-

Parkinson-White syndrome six months ago, she'd thought she faced her worst nightmare. The condition was an extra electrical pathway in the heart, which could cause a rapid, life-threateningly fast beat. The frustrating part was that nothing in particular seemed to set it off, and some people could go their entire lives without a significant episode or any need of treatment.

Her parents had never bothered to tell her she'd been followed for a heart condition when she was a child. How could they have withheld such vital information? After years of mild yet distressing symptoms, which she'd thought were anxiety attacks, she'd finally confronted them. They'd just shrugged their shoulders as if to say, *You were a preemie—what could we expect but that you'd have problems?*

Even now she found it difficult to forgive them. And her parents had yet to forgive *her* for her mother's kidney damage.

The old nagging thought of her parents doubting her capabilities had always had Amanda fighting to prove herself her entire life. Ever since her premature birth, when no one had expected her to survive, right on through her high school graduation, when her mother and father had assumed she'd get a low-entry job instead of going to college, they'd doubted her.

She shoved the hurtful thoughts back into a distant corner of her mind, needing to concentrate instead on the fact she was having more palpitations.

It had taken her internist over a year and several tests to pinpoint the real source of her frequent palpitations, and showing up in ER with a heart rate of two hundred beats a minute had finally clinched it.

Amanda took several slow, cleansing breaths, then performed the Valsalva maneuver by holding her breath and bearing down. This trick was known to slow down the pulse. She couldn't control WPW once it started any more than she could stop the sun from rising, but she tried to preempt it with the Valsalva maneuver. Once the heart impulses got on the wrong path, the pre-excitation beats rapidly marched on through, until they either mysteriously stopped on their own or an external electrical shock in the ER stopped them.

Tonight, if it went that far, she hoped for the mysterious former version, never wanting to go through the process of cardioversion again.

Maybe she should tell Hunter about her condition? But if she did, he'd treat her just like her parents did—as if she was fragile and incapable of handling her job and life. No. She'd keep her personal problems to herself for now. They were no concern of his.

There was one surefire way to fix WPW. She shuddered at the thought. It was invasive, and she definitely didn't want that procedure. Especially after the time she'd sent a twenty-one-year-old patient off for electrophysiology studies—EPS: a similar procedure to what she'd need—and the normally routine test had ended in disaster. He'd died on the table. Coupled with her mother's angiogram experience—another similar study—Amanda had become extremely hesitant about ever fixing her heart. Besides, her internist had promised that most people with WPW lived normal lives and rarely had episodes of severe tachycardia.

Nervously pulling at her sweatshirt, she clutched tight, until she realized the rapid beats had disappeared. Her heart rate was back to normal. Maybe the Valsalva had helped?

She took another deep breath, loosened her death grip on her shirt, and checked her pulse through the next minute. Yep. She was back to normal. Thank heavens.

# CHAPTER FIVE

THE next morning, at the Serena Vista Clinic parking lot, Hunter looked particularly attractive in his running attire. His shirt fit tight across his chest and hinted at the muscles Amanda had witnessed firsthand the other night in her living room. She swallowed and pretended she didn't notice him. Instead, she led the class through a brief stretch and warm-up routine, using a piece of music he'd suggested. It reminded her of an old boxing movie she'd seen in reruns on TV, but the musical theme definitely pumped her up.

Everyone smiled as they went through the exercises, which made her grin—until her eyes settled on Hunter. Again. He was a picture of near perfection, lunging and stretching his long hamstrings.

After last night's scare, though there was never anything in particular that would set off WPW, her fear of developing symptoms again made her decide to take it easy.

"Hunter," she said, edging him off to the side of the class, "will you take the joggers?"

"Why the sudden change in plan?"

"I'm feeling a little under the weather."

Several small groups had assembled around the parking lot. One group chatted, another stretched, and a third laughed along with the class clown, Jack Howling.

"What's wrong? Are you sick?"

"Nothing like that. I'm just a little tired, that's all."

"Maybe if you'd cut your schedule down and eat more regularly," he said out of the corner of his mouth so no one else could hear, "you'd have more energy."

"I promise to take the joggers out on Monday."

He searched her eyes, as if performing a lie-detector test, and after a long and hard stare, he gave a conciliatory nod.

Relieved she didn't have to explain anything more, she nodded back.

"Thanks," she said. And before he had a chance to think of any more questions, she read aloud the list of names for each group.

After she'd finished, he approached her and whispered coarsely, "What am I supposed to do with Sophie?"

His niece sat in her stroller, wearing a ridiculously sweet sunbonnet and baby sunglasses, which tied behind her head so she couldn't take them off. How did they make sunglasses so small? She'd tried her best to ignore how adorable the baby was, but today it was impossible. Just looking at her made Amanda's heart swell.

"You mean sweet pea?" she said.

Sophie slapped at the large colorful beads on her stroller bar, making them spin round and round to her delight. The sight made Amanda grin.

Hunter smiled back at her. "She does look extra cute today." Turning his gaze, and growing serious, he cased Amanda from head to toe. She was wearing her tried-and-true gray sweatsuit again, leaving *everything* to his imagination. "Don't change the subject. What about Sophie?"

"I'll take her," she said as though it would be a huge chore.

"Hey, Doc." Jack Howling, a well-built fifty-year-old with

more California-blond hair than gray, approached. "I wanted to tell you how much I like my CD. It really gets me jazzed up, you know?"

Hunter nodded and grinned. "That's good news."

"How about making one for nighttime?" another participant, Wendy, said. "I could use some help getting to sleep."

"I'd be glad to help you with that," Jack said, wiggling his eyebrows and making the attractive middle-aged woman blush.

"That's a great idea," Hunter said. "About the nighttime CD, I mean. I'll work on it at home this weekend."

The weekend.

What was Amanda supposed to do about the weekend? They hadn't discussed it when he'd moved in, but it only made sense that he'd return to his own house on the weekends. Fortunately, at the moment she was too distracted to think much about it.

"Okay, everyone." She cupped her hands around her mouth and spoke loud enough to catch their ears. Several people had fanned out across the parking lot. Once she was satisfied she had their undivided attention, she read the joggers' names off her clipboard, followed by the walkers' names, and they gathered into their assigned groups.

Hunter stepped in front of the joggers and began to run in place. His finely muscled calves and thighs tightened with each step. "Are we ready?"

They responded with a group hoot.

Some of the walkers looked to be in better condition than the joggers, but the groups had been divided scientifically by heart health and stamina, not physique. And looks could be deceiving. Even though slim and fit, a person could still have the cholesterol level of congealed fat and arterial plaque similar to the hard-water buildup in copper pipes.

"Let's go," Hunter called out.

He led the way, with his narrow hips and tight butt, and Amanda almost wished she were going with his group.

Glancing down at her baggy sweats, she tried her best not to feel frumpy. She assessed her walkers, mostly ladies, but a few men included. Physical training was new to many of them, and it could save their lives. All she needed to do was get them hooked on the positive effect of daily exercise. "Okay, folks, check your pulses." She waited while everyone did as told. "Let's give our hearts a workout!"

Stepping up behind Sophie's stroller, she took the lead with wide strides and a determined spirit, to whip these folks into shape over the remaining five weeks. Glancing over her shoulder, she saw they looked ready and willing to go along with the plan.

Sophie squealed with delight, and once again Amanda couldn't help but smile. That kid was so darn cute. She'd resisted the little one's charms for more than three days, and had done a fairly good job of it, but something about the sunshine and her little hat made all Amanda's barriers tumble down. A recurring thought about how quiet the house would be without her gave Amanda a pang of emptiness. How would she handle being alone on the weekend?

Two hours later, when the exercise portion of the day was complete, Amanda was still in her sweats and Hunter in his jogging gear. They worked in tandem to take and record blood pressures, pulses and short EKG strips for each participant. All the information would need to be uploaded into the computer, analyzed and compared with the prior data.

They tried not to get in each other's way, but due to the large group and small room it couldn't be helped.

After they'd dismissed everyone for lunch, they headed back to the office.

"Oh, excuse me," Amanda said, coming face to chest with Hunter and feeling a subtle hum of energy.

"Let me get that for you." He reached for several charts slipping from her grasp.

Why did she allow herself to look into his eyes? Did he know what he was doing, seducing her with his tilted head and moony charming glance? Was it all in her imagination, or was he playing her?

Whatever it was, she'd put a stop to it—as soon as he quit looking at her. In the meantime, she skirted around him and kept walking backward.

His gaze grew alert. "Ah?" He raised his hand and gestured to the right.

She finally broke eye contact and discovered she'd almost walked into a wall instead of out the office door. With her cheeks warming up, she glared at Hunter. "I'm going to run home and shower during lunch," she said, dropping the charts on her desk and scuttling out of the office.

"Don't forget to eat something," he called after her. "And record it!"

Amanda came back to the clinic after lunch for the group discussion session wearing her favorite black pants and a white cotton stretch top that hugged her in all the right places. She'd even taken her hair down.

The change hadn't gone unnoticed by her mentor, judging by the look on his freshly scrubbed face.

Hunter must have found the doctors' lounge and cleaned up while she'd been gone. His dark hair was still wet, and he was back in his black trousers and forest-green button-up shirt, though he'd forgone the tie. He'd rolled the sleeves halfway up his forearms, and looked dead serious gorgeous.

She glanced around the classroom and realized, even though most of the women were in their forties and older, she hadn't been the only one noticing Hunter's spectacular looks.

Amanda made time in the afternoon to go over the diet journals with each participant, and while she did that Hunter led a venting session where the patients could vocalize their concerns or fears. Later, she'd transcribe significant statements and include them with each participant's file.

"What if I go through all of this rigmarole and nothing changes?" one stout older man asked.

"You'll still be better off," Hunter replied. "Because your behavior will be modified and over the long haul an active person is a healthier person."

"Did you know that it takes three weeks for a routine to become a habit?" Jack Howling spoke up. The other man shook his head. "We're breaking old negative patterns and replacing them with positive life changes that will stick. Don't you think, Doc?"

"Absolutely," Hunter replied.

She loved every minute of being engrossed in her study—until she glanced at Hunter and remembered he'd packed his suitcase and Sophie's portable bed that morning. He planned on going home, and she'd be alone again.

Instead of being relieved, Amanda brushed the thought from her mind and distracted herself by sending everyone away with instructions for the weekend. Once they'd left, Amanda and Hunter transferred all the data back to the office.

"I'm thinking I'll cut out early and leave around three to beat the Friday-afternoon traffic, if that's okay with you?" Hunter plopped a stack of charts onto his desk.

Amanda covered her disappointment by doing the one trick

she knew. Using a pencil from her desk, she wove it over and under her knuckles with ease, back and forth, as if nothing at all bothered her. "I'm sure Sophie would like to sleep in her own crib for a change," she said.

"I've got some test results from one of my patients that will need my attention on Saturday, and Jade gets to make a phone call home on Sunday," he added, as if to justify his absence.

She tapped the eraser tip on the desk. "Tell her hi for me."

"Will do." He edged closer and placed his hand on her wrist to stop the escalating tapping.

"Sorry." Now her foot started jiggling, to make up for the nervous energy.

"Something bothering you?"

"No." She exaggerated the word, shook her head and rolled her eyes. She felt like a kid denying the truth. Why hadn't she prepared herself for his plans to go home? How had he managed to move into her world and throw everything off-kilter in such record time? It only made sense that he'd go home on the weekend, yet she'd let it take her by surprise.

According to Jack Howling, it took three weeks for a routine to become a habit, and she and Hunter had agreed to live together until Jade came home...for Sophie's sake. The realization made what little she'd had for lunch turn into a hard ball in her stomach. In three weeks, everyone else in the Mending Hearts Club study might be better off, but what about her?

"Do you want to send some of this data home with me, so I can help?" he asked.

"No." There was that breathy, overembellished response again, as though his offer to help was absurd. Fact was, she was depending on the work to keep her occupied. "I was planning on spending the weekend doing that, and hopefully I'll be able to start the journal article, too."

"Aren't you scheduling any downtime? Going to a movie with a friend, or eating out or something?"

"I promised myself if the grant came through I'd give my all to make sure this project was a success. I knew going in that I'd be working nonstop, pulling it all together. So for now my social life is nonexistent."

Little did Hunter know that her social life had been pretty much nonexistent long before the study had begun. But that was an ongoing saga, and she never planned to bore him with the details. It would be too humiliating.

"And I'm still scheduled to work the Urgent Care unit on Saturday night." She did her best to sound cheery.

He gave an exaggerated and impressed nod. "Well, don't knock yourself out," he said, with a look she remembered as Hunter's version of subtle concern.

When three o'clock rolled around, Hunter packed up Sophie and let her give Amanda a sloppy kiss goodbye.

"Have a great weekend," he said, with a sincere smile and an encouraging wink.

"Sure will. You, too!" How phony did that sound?

And without a further word, Hunter whisked the baby away.

When Amanda walked through her door that evening, arms loaded with files and papers, she felt strangely depressed. Sophie had become a part of her life in less than a week. All the extra activity and sound had made her home come alive. Even with all her resistance to the baby, she'd brightened her world—a world Amanda hadn't realized had grown dull until she'd seen and felt the difference between living alone and living as a makeshift family. She immediately missed Sophie.

And Hunter.

It amazed her how his presence had filled up space so pleasantly, and how the house felt deadly quiet and empty now that he was gone. It felt too reminiscent of the time they'd separated. She shuddered at the memory.

She'd already grown used to his quiet tapping on the computer keyboard in his room. In the morning, she took comfort in hearing classical music play as he prepared for the day. Even his new scent lingered in her mind—a spicy fragrance she had quickly grown fond of in place of his old aftershave.

She walked into the guest bathroom and searched for the cologne. He'd taken it with him. Even so, she understood the bottled fragrance couldn't duplicate what his body added. Nope, that special touch of Hunter had definitely gone missing.

A furry stroke against her leg made her look down.

At least she still had Jinx.


Hunter took Amanda completely by surprise when he showed up at her house Sunday evening.

"Hope you don't mind," he said. "But I couldn't bear the thought of Monday-morning traffic."

Mandy squirmed on her doorstep, having been caught in jogging shorts and a skimpy T-shirt. Her hair was tied in a knot on the top of her head, and she didn't have a lick of makeup on. Why hadn't he called first?

"Thought I'd be smart and drive out this afternoon."

"You should have called. Let me know you were on your way." She wrapped her arms across her chest and held her shoulders. How obvious was that? If he hadn't noticed her braless state before, he was sure to now. She scratched her neck and did everything but look into his eyes.

"You're right. I'll call next time."

Sophie squealed. Thank goodness for the distraction.

"Hey, sweet pea, what's up?" she said.

"We going in?" he asked, looking exceptionally handsome in jeans and a tight, pale blue polo shirt left untucked.

"Sure."

Once she'd gotten over the combined shock and rush of seeing Hunter, Amanda admitted she was pleased to have them back at home. One huge question popped into her mind. Had he planned this?

"You know, if you're not doing anything tonight, I thought we could see a movie. Sophie would sleep through it, I'm sure."

A movie? How could she get out of that? "Only if I get to choose which one."

"Tell you what, you can choose the movie if you promise to have a large popcorn with it. Need to fatten you up."

"Do you have any idea how much salt there is in that?"

"And is there any reason you need to be on a two-gram sodium diet?"

They stared at each other. The moments yawned into seconds. What was he getting at? Did he have a clue about her? If she told him about her WPW diagnosis, it would only reinforce his image of her being weak and unable to juggle a challenging schedule and have a normal family life. He'd made it clear when they were married he didn't think she could cope with a child and a career. Why would his attitude have changed now? No. It was best to hold on to her secret a while longer—or until she'd proved herself to him.

"Okay. Popcorn it is. And we'll be seeing that new romantic comedy with that gorgeous British actor."

Hunter rolled his eyes as if he'd just been defeated at poker. Amanda couldn't help feeling pleased to have something to do besides stare at her empty computer screen the rest of the evening. She turned to go shower and change clothes.

Could it be Hunter had cooked up this arriving early scheme because he'd missed her as much as she'd missed him?

Nah. He was just being practical for Sophie's sake.

After a surprisingly relaxing evening out together, a carefully orchestrated game of hiding without seeking took place the next morning. Hunter and Amanda went about preparing for their second week by avoiding being in the same room with each other until they both showed up at the front door at the same time.

"Maybe we should carpool?" he said.

"I don't think it would be a good idea," she said, scrambling for her briefcase.

"Afraid someone might get the wrong impression?" He grinned at her with a twinkle in his eyes.

"Get over yourself, Phillips. I just think we need to keep a professional distance."

"Suit yourself," he said, opening the door and motioning for her to go first. Sophie, in her combination car seat/carrier, hung from his other arm and played with her toes. "Just seems kind of silly wasting the extra gas…"

"Oh, all right."

And, much to Amanda's chagrin, a new routine had begun.

Amanda and Hunter cooperated professionally all day at work, and when the evening rolled around, they respected each other's privacy. When Amanda skipped dinner and dove right into research and catching up with the statistics, he didn't criticize her. And she didn't tell him how to care for his niece…unless he asked.

Late on Wednesday morning, in a rare moment of downtime, Amanda fought off a grin at the sight of Hunter. He wore his white doctor's coat, and sat with his feet on the office desk with

Sophie wrapped in his arm. She wanted to snap a picture and title it *Man, baby, and a bottle*.

He'd leaned his head against the headrest and closed his eyes. The sound of Amanda taking her seat caused him to open them. "I never realized how relaxing feeding a baby could be."

"I hear nursing is as good as taking a sedative," she said, pulling out her drawer and fishing for a pen.

"That's one experience I'll have to miss. Darn."

Sophie sucked away and Hunter distractedly ran his fingers over her head, playing with her flyaway tufts of hair. The sight almost made Amanda's heart clutch. Where was that dang pen?

"You know," Hunter said, "I'm really impressed with this program of yours."

She stopped fishing for the pen and gave him a surprised glance.

"You seem so passionate about it. What made you develop the concept?"

Amanda closed the drawer and folded her hands on the desk. "My mom."

"Chloe actually encouraged you about something?"

"You sound as jaded as me," she said with a wry laugh.

"Well, I know your history."

She nodded. True. Hunter knew everything about her ongoing battle for respect from her parents.

"When my mom's doctor encouraged her to have an angiogram last year, I wholeheartedly agreed. Mom didn't want anything to do with it. She didn't care if she had plaque or a blockage. I had to convince her to sign the consent."

Hunter shifted Sophie from the crook of his arm to his chest to burp her. The peaceful sight contradicted the storm in Amanda's stomach.

"The ironic thing was, for once my parents listened to me

as a medical professional." She shook her head. "And where did it get them? Mom suffered severe kidney damage from the radiopaque dye used in the procedure."

"Surely they understood that was a fluke? Just bad luck and not anything you'd done?"

"You would think. But my father held me accountable for it, which feeds in beautifully to their ongoing lack of confidence in me, wouldn't you say?"

"Do you want me to have a word with them?" The tension in his voice made Sophie fuss. He patted her back and quieted both of them down.

"It's my battle, Hunter. I haven't given up on them. I'll work things out. Anyway, I got to thinking about helping people avoid the need for tests such as angiograms in the first place, giving people a more autonomous approach to their health, and voilà!"

He shook his head. "When are they ever going to learn what a gem you are?"

She raised her brows. "Wow, thanks."

"It's the truth."

They gazed at each other and Amanda let a temptingly familiar feeling creep in. Hunter had always supported her academic dreams.

Jack Howling came barreling into the room with a broad grin on his face. She was grateful for the distraction.

"Check this out." He shoved a newspaper into Amanda's hands. "There's an article about us. See? There we all are, jogging."

After almost giving in to her parents' brand of defeatist gloom, Amanda felt a welcome surge of pride as she read the headline. *Local Nurse Changes Lives*. Her smile stretched from ear to ear, and when she looked at Hunter, he mirrored her joy.

It had been a long time since someone had been in her corner, and even if it was only professionally, it felt damn good.

On Thursday night, Amanda could tell Hunter needed some time to himself. Sophie was fussy and pouting, and nothing he did could satisfy her.

"I've got an idea," Amanda said, sweeping up Sophie and twirling her around in the air. "Let's give Uncle Hunter a break." She smiled at him. "We're gonna have a girls' night." Sophie's little T-shirt had risen up, and Amanda blew on her belly. The baby laughed. "You're going to spend the night with me. How about that?" Sophie kicked her feet.

"Hey," Hunter said. "I can't let you do that."

"Sure you can. Just say yes."

Though he might not want to admit it, she could see the tension dissipate from his face. He knew a good offer when he heard one. And for such an independent man, he'd been tethered to his niece for two full weeks without a break. "Well, maybe just this once."

"Deal," she said, and high-fived him. Sophie squealed with delight.

And secretly, though Amanda knew she might be setting herself up for pain, she couldn't wait to have Sophie all to herself.

By the time the second weekend rolled around, though even more used to living as a makeshift family, Amanda steeled herself against being alone by delving into more research for her journal article.

This time, prepared for Hunter and Sophie's Sunday-night arrival, Amanda met them at the door in a sweatsuit.

When an extra shift at the UC clinic became available on the Monday night of the third week, Amanda snatched it up. Things had gotten a little too cozy with Hunter and Sophie, and even though he was paying rent, she still needed time away. Maybe it was a backlash against getting too close to him last week, or maybe self-defense, but working at Urgent Care became front and center in her new plan to avoid Hunter.

At eleven-thirty, her key was no sooner in the lock than the door flew open. Hunter looked surprised, but waved her inside.

"You scared me," she said.

"I'm sorry. I've been waiting for you."

Oh, no. She'd done her best to avoid him all day, and he'd been waiting for her? She didn't stand a chance. "Why?"

"Because tonight's the night," he said, a broad smile on his face.

"What's that supposed to mean?" She tingled as though a procession of kittens had advanced across her skin, but she resisted the subtle pleasure. At work today he hadn't alluded to tonight being anything special in the least. With her feet suddenly glued to the floor, she couldn't budge from the threshold. He coaxed her with a tug on her lab coat.

"Come on. I've got everything all set up."

She hesitated, but stepped inside. He closed the door and she felt completely alone with him, as though for the first time and in a completely different way. It made her nervous.

His gaze danced around her face. "You don't have a clue what tonight is, do you?" He couldn't hide his obvious disappointment.

"Not really." She shook her head, all the while skimming her memory for the significance of this particular early-August night. It wasn't her birthday. Or his. It wasn't their anniversary—and why would she even think about that?

"Every summer… Our favorite night…" He prompted smiling. "The Perseid meteor showers!"

There was a knock on the door. Hunter lunged around her to open it. A pizza delivery guy handed a delicious-smelling box over and Hunter gave him some money. "Keep the change," he said as he kicked the door shut with his foot. "I thought you were the pizza guy. That's why I jumped on the door." He hoisted the box on his fingertips. "While we're watching the stars, I thought I'd do my part to fatten you up, too." He grabbed her hand and led the way toward the sliding glass doors.

She worried her hand felt clammy, but followed him outside to her patio, where he'd set everything up. The table had been set complete with champagne glasses, and her best dishes and flatware, just like they'd always used to on their big meteor-watching night.

It seemed like ancient history—an era that had long since been forgotten in the archives of her life. The thought of annual meteor showers hadn't crossed her mind in three years. Had she shed all of life's simple pleasures when they'd broken up?

"Don't worry," he said, making her think she should worry. He sounded like an excited kid. "I didn't forget to order pine-apple and Canadian bacon on your half."

Amanda really did like Canadian bacon and pineapple on her pizza, even if it was way off her self-imposed low-sodium diet. And he'd remembered. She hadn't forgotten that the last time she'd had Hawaiian pizza was with Hunter, in her prior life.

Maybe just a piece or two would be okay.

She put her purse and lab coat down and shook her head at the situation, her resistance to the notion of stargazing with Hunter slowly melting. Why not? He'd gone to great lengths to organize everything, not to mention to make a big deal out of one of their former rituals. Admitting it felt nice, she sat down just as he popped the cork on the champagne and poured some into her glass.

"Thank you." She smiled, feeling the hint of a chill all over her body, even though it was still a comfortable eighty degrees outside.

"Wait," he said, before she could take a sip. "First a toast."

He lifted his cup. She joined him. "When I was a little kid, my favorite teacher at boarding school used to tell me that I'd get a wish for each shooting star I saw." He glanced at her, mischief sparkling in his gaze. "Tonight I hope we see hundreds of shooting stars, and that all of our wishes come true," he said, in a thick, intimate voice.

With his intense and deep-set eyes probing her, a picture formed in her mind of the night he'd asked her to marry him. The only thing that had changed was his now rugged and intriguing nose. *And* the fact he'd suddenly become Dr. Dad. For some dumb reason, his face started to go blurry. She'd always been a sucker for Hunter's earnest toasts. Hoping he wouldn't notice, she lifted her glass and practically drained it.

He'd taken an ordinary occasion and turned it into the most special night of her life since she'd been with him. Did he have any idea how socially starved she was? How much he was torturing her?

When he served her a slice of pizza, she took a big bite and burned the roof of her mouth. Desperately needing to break the mood, she said, with a droll smile and her mouth full, "You realize we're going to have to record this in our diet journals?"

Hunter nodded and grinned at Mandy, before folding his pizza slice in half and taking a huge bite. She looked great, sitting on the patio with starlight in her hair. He could have sworn her eyes had teared up during the toast. He nursed a tender feeling for a beat or two, but decided not to go maudlin on the poor unsuspecting woman.

"When we share our journals with the Mending Hearts Club, they'll understand we're not perfect," he said as he shoved another large bite into his mouth, savoring every spicy and cheesy taste. "And, like you said to the class, everything in moderation. Right?"

"What if they catch on that we had dinner together?" she asked.

"Nah. Everyone eats pizza. Besides, my half is meatball and pepperoni. Trust me, no one's going to figure out we're living together from our diet journals."

As minimally reassuring as that sounded, she relaxed and enjoyed the rest of her pizza.

After they'd finished eating, Hunter refilled their glasses and turned off the lights. The meteor showers were the perfect excuse to get closer—physically closer.

That morning while he'd shaved, he'd heard a brief announcement on the radio about the Perseid showers. All kinds of memories had rushed through his head, and he'd made the plan on his drive out to the Serena Vista Clinic.

He'd always been goal-oriented, and after spending a couple of weeks with Mandy, he'd realized how much he was still attracted to her. Hell, he'd realized that right off, but with each passing day he'd craved her a bit more—until now he flat out wanted her. The thoughts wouldn't go away and practically drove him crazy. He wanted her back in his bed. Tonight he'd decided to take the first step.

Why couldn't they have a sexual relationship without getting involved? People seemed to do it all the time. And they were living together. Could it get any more convenient?

Now, setting the scene, he moved their chairs to the edge of the patio, from where they could see the full night sky, and invited Mandy to sit. Even with the city lights drowning out thousands of distant stars, there were plenty left to see, and they were in luck with a new moon.

"Wait. I forgot something." He rushed inside for his portable CD player, checked quickly on Sophie sleeping away, selected a special symphony, and sprinted back outside as if he'd missed a million meteors in his absence.

"You've thought of everything," Mandy said, quaffing the last of her drink and looking decidedly more relaxed.

Gustav Holst's "The Planets" seemed like the perfect choice. He pushed Play and felt as though they were embarking on a space cruise, just the two of them.

"The meteor shower should be over there," he said, pointing to the northeast section of the sky just as a meteor streaked past.

"Ooh," Mandy cooed. "Did you see that?"

He nodded and reached for her, and noticed she didn't put up much of a fight. He put his arm around her shoulders. "Did you make a wish?"

"I forgot," she said.

Soon she'd hooked her thumb through his belt loop, giving him a contented rush. She hadn't put her arm around his waist, as he would have preferred, but it was progress. Together they stood for several minutes, waiting for another meteor to shoot by.

Her wonder matched his awe at the sight of the seemingly endless heavens, and they shared a special thrill when two meteors streaked past within seconds of each other.

Knowing it was just a kids' game, Hunter still made a double wish. He stole a glance at Mandy's pert profile, while resisting the impulse to touch the tip of her nose. She relaxed against him, and he thought one of his wishes had already come true. But this was no game. This was potential sex with the ex, which could backfire into an explosion of meteoric proportions if he didn't handle things delicately.

An hour, ten shooting stars and an equal number of wishes later, they decided to call it a night. Tuesday was another full day, and Hunter suspected that Mandy hadn't gotten nearly enough rest over the weekend.

"Good thing we don't have to be at the clinic until nine tomorrow," he said, clearing off the patio table.

She glanced up from helping him and smiled warmly. "Thank you for this, Hunter. I'd forgotten how special meteor showers are." She walked toward him and leaned close, as if to touch his cheek. Had another wish been granted? No way would he waste this perfect opportunity. He moved forward to meet her.

Their lips met.

He caressed her arms to keep her from backing away. Her mouth was as soft as he remembered. Warm and inviting. She pressed her lips to his. Dizzy with desire and his good fortune, he forced restraint. The tender kiss was no mistake. It gave him hope for millions more. Her arms relaxed and she surrendered when he parted her lips and touched the tip of her tongue. She tasted tart and sinful, just like the champagne. A tiny moan escaped her throat—a sound that used to drive him crazy. It still did. Wanting to devour her and rip off her clothes, he broke away before he lost control. He'd have to take things slow and gradual to get her back to his bed. Tonight he'd have to settle for a single kiss.

Heady with her flavor, he focused on her eyes, softened with wonder. But her mood quickly changed. He felt it before he could see it under the dim patio lantern.

Fire flamed in her aquamarine stare. She bit her lower lip as though protecting it. "That wasn't a good idea," she said, and she broke from his grasp and headed for the door.

Everything had changed in the glimpse of a moment. Quicker than a shooting star.

# CHAPTER SIX

MANDY disappeared down the hall and shut the door. To Hunter, it felt like a slap in the face.

Talk about misjudging her actions… He'd thought her leaning into him while they watched the night sky had meant they were on the same wavelength. He shouldn't have moved so quickly, but she'd gazed so trustingly up into his eyes, and she'd looked so damn beautiful he hadn't been able to stop himself. But he'd been thinking with his *other* brain. He couldn't take back what had happened—and, remembering their kiss, he didn't want to.

He'd been foolish to think they could have a purely physical relationship. Even if she agreed to sex, how could he trust she wouldn't suddenly change her mind? He'd believed her with all his heart when they'd married and she'd said her career and their marriage were all she ever wanted. That sure as hell had backfired. No, she couldn't be trusted. Come to think of it, he was *lucky* she'd refused him tonight. It would save both of them a whole lot of confusion and added headache in the long run. And though it wasn't obvious that Mandy still wanted children, he suspected by the sparkle in her eyes whenever she was with Sophie that she still longed to be a mother. And he definitely never wanted to be a father. Bottom line—nothing had changed between them. Unfortunately not even the sexual attraction.

For survival's sake he'd play it safe, keep his distance, do everything by the book, and follow her cautions about treating her like any other coworker—maybe even move to the extended-stay hotel. But above all he'd pretend tonight had never happened. It might not be that special sexy wish he'd conjured up, but if playing it safe was what Mandy expected of him, that was what he'd give her.

He heard water filling her bathtub. He hadn't been above sneaking a peek at her bathroom before, and he knew she had a sunken tub.

Losing the ability to keep his mind clear, he couldn't help his X-rated thoughts of Mandy removing her clothes and standing before him naked. He remembered her breasts and how they felt when he lavished them with attention. He envisioned the curve of her hips and the splash of hair at the V where her long legs came together. The thought of her staggered his mind. His body flushed and his heart sped up.

This was torture, pure and simple. In order to survive he had to move to a hotel.

Hunter shook the images from his head, trying to distract himself. He strode toward the kitchen sink and cleaned like a madman, taking his frustration out on the job at hand. After he'd washed the dishes, he feverishly scrubbed down the countertops and put away the leftover pizza. He forced himself to think of other things, like salvaging their rekindled friendship, but the sunken tub and Mandy kept coming to mind.

When he was done in the kitchen, he tucked the dish towel into the rack and headed down the hall for bed.

As if a masochist, Hunter slowed his pace and stopped outside Mandy's door. Quiet New Age music played in the master bedroom. She was playing the CD he'd made to help the Mending Hearts Club go to sleep.

What would he use to help himself go to sleep?

He reached out and touched the doorknob. It felt warm and, like a crystal ball, planted an image in his brain. He saw Mandy reclining in the large deep tub, surrounded by candles flickering and dancing on the walls. Which essential oil fragrance had she dripped into the water? Lavender? White rose blossom?

How warm and inviting the water would be. He imagined sliding into the tub across from her, fondling her thighs with his feet, pulling her to his chest, her high pert breasts resting on him, heaven on earth. How would she feel after all these years, skin to skin, if she wrapped her long legs around his waist? His hands would grasp her glorious backside and savor the feel as he moved her closer. How would the delicate skin on her neck taste? Would she arch her back? Would she purr when his hands danced over her body? How would she smell when he toweled off every centimeter of her satin skin before leading her to bed?

How would she feel when he penetrated her?

The doorknob fired up under his grasp, sending liquid heat up his arm, fanning out over his chest and settling into a rushing molten river in his gut. His heart hammered in his chest. He tightened his grip on the knob and began to turn—but yanked away in one lightning-quick jerk. Stepping back, he took a deep breath.

After several moments of recovery and contemplation, he promised himself that whatever had overcome him tonight couldn't be allowed to happen again.

At least not just yet. For both their sakes.

He tapped lightly on the door.

"Yes?"

He clenched his jaw to keep from saying what he desperately wanted. That he'd never gotten over her. He swallowed back the words and kept his voice steady. "Just wanted to say good-night."

There was a pause. He waited as the silence gripped like a vise around his heart.

"Things are different now, Hunter. We can't go back."

He wanted to yell, *Why not?* Instead, he tipped his forehead to the door and squinted at the reality that it might be too late for them to reclaim any kind of relationship, let alone casual sex. Nothing about Mandy could ever be completely carefree. They'd both been burned and had the scars to prove it.

"Good night," came her muffled voice.

With a heavy sigh, he placed the palm of his hand against the wood. It felt cold. "Good night," he whispered.

Three in the morning and Sophie woke with a vengeance. Hunter jumped out of bed and gathered her up in his arms. She knotted her fists and kicked her legs, crying as if in excruciating pain. He checked and changed her diaper, but she wouldn't quiet down.

"Shh...shh," he whispered by her ear, cuddling and gently bouncing her. She wailed harder.

He walked her to the kitchen to prepare a bottle while she continued to howl. "You're okay," he chanted, over and over.

She kept crying, letting him know she definitely wasn't.

Trying to console a baby while fixing a bottle was awkward at best, but with Sophie's nonstop squirming, he was worried he'd spill the formula, or drop the bottle—or, worse yet, drop her.

Hunter fumbled on.

"Do you need any help?" Mandy asked.

"Oh," he said, surprised. He'd been so distracted with Sophie, he hadn't heard her come in. "Could you make a bottle for me?" He wrapped his now free hand around Sophie and started pacing and lightly bouncing while he rubbed her back and kissed her head. Her wisps of hair tickled his cheek. When had she come to be so precious to him?

Elephant-sized tears streaked down her cheeks and it pained him. He felt her head. She was warm from shrieking, but not feverish. Relief washed away his fear that she might be sick.

"Are you getting another tooth? What's wrong, sugar?" Never in his life had he felt so useless. His heart ached for the squalling baby, but he hadn't a clue what the hell was bothering her. Nearly three weeks as a surrogate caregiver hadn't made him any wiser. He continued on with his failing method to soothe her.

"Let me have her." Mandy held out her arms, holding the bottle.

Relieved at the break, Hunter handed Sophie over.

"You miss your mommy, don't you, sweet pea?" she said with all the compassion in the world. Sophie slapped the bottle away and wrapped her arms around Mandy's neck. She walked her round and round the dining table, humming a nursery rhyme.

"Mm, mm, mum, mm," Sophie cried, though quieter now. "Mm, mm, mum, mm. Mum-mum-mumm."

"Is she saying what I think she is?" Hunter asked, picking up the bottle.

"Honestly? I think it's too early for her to know that word. I think she's just comforting herself."

"Looks like you've got the magic touch," he said, wiping off the nipple and offering the bottle to Sophie one more time.

Mandy cuddled her close and kissed her cheek, then wiped Sophie's nose with a tissue she'd miraculously made appear from her robe pocket. Sophie reached for the bottle, and Mandy found a chair and made herself comfortable to feed the baby.

She'd taken over the job and had been able to do what he couldn't: console a baby who missed her momma. He shoved his fingers through his hair, feeling exasperated and tense.

Sophie started to fuss again.

"I think she's picking up on your frustration, Hunter. Calm down. She's okay."

He took a deep breath, bewildered that he could have such an impact on a baby. "Mandy, I'm so sorry we woke you up. I can usually quiet her down fine, but this time she seemed so…so distraught. Do you really think it's because Jade's gone?"

Mandy shrugged and cooed to the baby while she sipped at her bottle. "Who can be sure about anything?"

Sophie's eyes opened and closed, as though she was fighting off sleep. Mandy held her close to her breast and stroked her cheek until finally the heavy lids stayed shut. She looked up and smiled at Hunter. Victory.

The picture knocked him off balance. She was a natural at mothering. He'd fought her when she'd told him she wanted a baby, even accused her of being incapable of caring for a houseplant let alone a baby. She'd missed her period and had an epiphany. Hunter had thought it was a tidy ending and a stroke of good luck when she'd finally gotten back on her cycle. He'd insisted they'd agreed to never have kids when they'd married. And what about her PhD? He'd tried to distract and bribe her with her next degree. But now she wouldn't settle for anything less than a family. He couldn't let himself open up to the pain a family could bring. He'd learned only too well with his own parents how devastating neglect and indifference could be. He couldn't allow his sexual attraction to Mandy to trip him up into changing his mind about life, love and families.

"I can't keep disrupting your life," he said, filled with concern. "Tomorrow Sophie and I will move to a hotel."

"Please don't, Hunter. Not if it's on my account. I love having Sophie here."

That was what he was concerned about—his niece putting all kinds of silly baby dreams into her thoughts again.

Mandy kissed the baby's head, then laid her cheek against it. She smiled at him. "And in case you're still thinking about what happened earlier, I loved watching the stars with you tonight. Truth is, no one has been remotely as thoughtful as you for a long time, and it meant a lot to me."

He forced a smile, but all he wanted to do was hold her. If he could take her into his arms and bury himself inside her, maybe all the confusion would go away. But was it really only about sex?

"Just no more kissing, okay?"

*What?* He tilted his head, weighing the options. The expression on her face was less than convincing. She'd said she loved having Sophie around, but what about him?

"Hunter?"

"Okay. We'll stay," he said, purposely avoiding committing to the "no more kissing" part.

Amanda and Hunter maintained a friendly yet cool professionalism over the remainder of the week and into the fourth week. They were cooperative and helpful to each other, but beyond class hours and being with Sophie spent little time together. When she wasn't working the UC to avoid him, Amanda holed up in her room most nights, entering data into the computer and writing her article. Hunter caught up on his medical journal reading, and bringing his patient files up to date.

They took turns caring for Sophie, and were the picture of domestic partnership—except for the fact that they tiptoed around each other, trying to deny the passion that still existed between them. Hunter wished he could find a way to put an end to their tortured truce, but he'd settle for whatever he could take if it meant spending time with Mandy. He'd missed her that much.

With Jade set to be released after the coming weekend, he needed to plan and make his next move sooner than Mandy might be ready.

As the week went on, Hunter received unfortunate results on the thyroid scan for Mrs. Peters. The matter required a face-to-face appointment to discuss the options. Since his patient lived just as close to the Serena Vista Clinic—which was owned by Mercy Hospital—as she did to his home base clinic, on Thursday evening he'd planned to meet her at Serena Vista Urgent Care. He'd arranged to have doctor privileges there at the satellite clinic for one night.

While he waited, he agreed to see a few walk-in patients.

One patient, according to his records, had been to the UC every other night for the past two weeks. He was being treated for a lung abscess on home intravenous therapy, but his peripheral heplock IVs kept failing after a day or two of treatment. The last vein had lasted only a day and had developed phlebitis. What he needed was a peripherally inserted central catheter, and Hunter knew the perfect nurse—who'd just happened to take another shift that night—to do it.

"Dr. Phillips has ordered a PICC line and wants you to do the honors," Amanda's friend Marian said.

"What the heck is *he* doing here?"

Hunter had never worked at the Serena Vista Clinic before. No sooner had Amanda said it than he appeared at the nurses' station from an exam room.

Years before, when Marian had already been a nurse practitioner and Amanda had been working at Mercy Hospital on the evening shift, the three of them used to go out for drinks after work. Marian had been the person responsible for convincing Amanda to take the next step in her nursing education.

"He's just as hot as he used to be," Marian whispered before waving hello to Hunter and sashaying away.

Amanda rolled her eyes, then composed herself and turned toward Hunter. "You need a PICC line?"

"Yes. You're still certified, right?"

"Sure am. Where's Sophie?"

"I asked Louise if she could watch her for a couple of hours."

Louise was one of the Mending Hearts Club participants, who flipped out her grandchildren's pictures at the drop of a hat. She'd bonded with Sophie the very first night of class.

"How nice of her," she said, thinking how the group had quickly changed from being mere subjects in her study to something more. "Okay, then." Amanda scratched her upper lip. "Has the patient been moved to the procedure room?"

"I'm on it," a nearby medical assistant said. She grabbed a wheelchair and headed toward the exam room, to collect the patient and push him down the hall to the procedure room.

Amanda searched the clinic for the portable ultrasound machine, and after gathering the items she'd need for the PICC line, headed toward the procedure room.

"I'll help you," Hunter said, following behind.

After Mr. Paredes had been placed on a gurney, Amanda introduced herself and explained exactly what she intended to do. While she washed her hands, Hunter set up the ultrasound machine and searched the patient's upper arm for the brachial vein Amanda would need to locate.

"Thanks," Amanda said.

"No problem," Hunter said, before turning to Mr. Paredes. "Mandy's an excellent nurse. She'll numb you up and you won't feel a thing."

Amanda went through all the normal protocol for starting an IV in the bend of a patient's left elbow, the antecubital fossa, and gently injected a small amount of numbing medicine. After inserting a small needle into the large vein, using sterile technique, she inserted an introducer needle and, with the help of the ultrasound, guided the PICC line into the superior vena cava—the vein nearest his heart.

"Looks good," Hunter said. "Let's get an AP of the chest to make sure."

Within a few minutes, the portable chest X-ray tech appeared and took the picture. A few minutes later Hunter discerned that the PICC line was properly placed.

Once she got the nod, Amanda injected more numbing medicine into Mr. Paredes's arm and sutured the line in place, then put a clear sterile dressing and a pressure bandage on top of that.

"You'll need to come back tomorrow night to have the dressing changed," she said. "But after that we'll teach you how to care for the PICC line yourself, and it should be smooth sailing."

He nodded gratefully.

"Dr. Phillips?" an MA called from the doorway. "That patient you're expecting is here."

"Thanks," he said. "Mandy, I'm probably going to do a thyroid needle biopsy on Mrs. Peters. Will you assist me?"

A familiar feeling of how it had used to be at Mercy Hospital took Amanda by surprise. Without trying she and Hunter had fallen back into a routine at home, and now the same was happening at the clinic. Truth was, they worked well together, and she enjoyed assisting him.

"Of course. Call me when you're ready. I'll finish up here and get everything together."

Fifteen minutes later, after prepping the patient, Amanda

watched Hunter skillfully perform a biopsy from the thyroid nodule by inserting a tiny needle into the base of the throat and drawing out a thread-sized core of tissue, almost too small to see. Judging by the patient's reaction, it was relatively painless. Amanda held the specimen container for him to submerge the needle biopsy in. She then carefully labeled the specimen and hand-carried it to the clinic lab for courier shipment to the main Mercy Hospital laboratory for pathologic examination the next day.

Hunter had requested a STAT report, and she suspected it was to confirm his worst suspicions. The only remaining question would be which type of thyroid cancer it would be.

As she was on her way in to examine another walk-in patient, Hunter stopped her at the door. "Thanks for all your help tonight."

"Oh, no problem. It's what I do."

He nodded. "And you're fantastic at it."

They gazed wordlessly at each for a few moments, and she wondered what he was thinking. Hunter had always been supportive of her job—that had never been their problem—but when it came to her wanting a family, he'd balked.

"You know, if you pursue your PhD in nursing, it will relegate you to teaching or research, and you won't have nearly as much patient contact. Are you sure that's what you want?"

Okay, so she hadn't had to wait long to find out what he'd been thinking. And, damn it, he made a good point. But she was prepared with her answer. She'd thought a lot about it already. "I may not have the same amount of patient contact, but I'll be able to reach a larger scope of patients through my studies. I know you think I'm out to prove my parents and the world wrong about me, but the most important part about the Mending Hearts Club isn't me, it's helping the participants turn their lives around."

"I know what you're saying, Mandy. But you'll miss the one-on-one contact. I know that much about you."

She studied her nursing logs and thought how much she enjoyed caring for her patients. He was right.

"Well, I'm going to pick up Sophie and take her back to your house," he said. "See you later. I might already be in bed when you get home."

The MA was nearby, and Amanda couldn't help but notice her lifted brows and sudden elevated interest in the conversation. Great. Now a fact they'd been careful to keep hidden for professional reasons—that they were living together—would be all over the clinic by morning.

But it wasn't like that. Amanda could hear herself doing damage control, explaining over and over to people who would already have made up their minds about them living under the same roof. She didn't really care what anyone thought about her personally, but she didn't want any gossip to detract from the importance of the Mending Hearts Club project.

We're not sleeping together, she told herself. And yet with the way her feelings for Hunter had been running from warm to boiling hot lately, she wondered how long that was going to be true.

Friday morning, Amanda gathered her joggers and set out for a thirty-minute run. The sun burned hot in typical mid-August fashion.

"Be sure to drink lots of water," she said, raising her own bottle and taking a swig.

Sweat beaded quickly on the men, and the women glistened with moisture by the time they hit their third pass around the public track. Across the park, Amanda spotted Hunter and his group of walkers.

The Mending Hearts Club waved and cheered each other on from the other side of the green, having bonded and formed new friendships over the past few weeks.

Jack Howling, always good for a laugh, picked up speed with a silly-looking run, and pulled ahead as though showing off for one of the women. Though Jack's cholesterol and blood pressure had been high at the beginning of the study, his EKG was normal and his stress test had been outstanding. And he was a natural athlete. By following the heart-healthy diet, Amanda predicted his next cholesterol test would show marked improvement. This morning his blood pressure and pulse before the run had been well within the normal range, and exercise was the perfect way to help him elevate his good cholesterol—the high-density lipoprotein.

Now running full stride, he widened the gap between him and the group.

"Show-off!" she chided with a grin.

Well ahead of the group, he pretended to trip, and she grinned wider. What a ham. When he stumbled, she thought he was going overboard with the playacting.

Then he fell.

She rushed to catch up to him. "Get Dr. Phillips!" she called over her shoulder to the group. "Jack!" she yelled. He didn't respond. She leveled her face close to his and watched his chest. It didn't rise, and she couldn't feel any air passing through his nose. A quick shake of his shoulder and a check of the carotid artery proved what she feared most—he was unconscious because his heart had stopped beating.

She positioned his head to open his airway and breathed for him, then began chest compressions. His skin was already cool and clammy and she suspected the worst—that he'd had a massive heart attack.

Within a minute, Hunter had skidded to a stop next to her. "Noreen has her cell phone. She's calling 9-1-1." He relieved her of the job of external compressions.

They worked together as a team, doing two-man CPR, focusing only on the patient, and willing him to survive until the paramedics arrived with their equipment. *Come on, Jack, don't give up.* Her heart ached for him. A few minutes and several rounds of CPR later, much to her relief she heard a siren in the distance.

Amanda could only imagine how shocked the others would be at the sight of the fittest participant sprawled out on the park sidewalk. But she couldn't stop what she was doing. Jack's life depended on it.

She glanced at Hunter after giving two more quick breaths. Expertly he made sure their patient's blood still circulated through his heart by making deep and even compressions. She could feel the artificial pulse under her fingertips placed over Jack's carotid artery.

The ambulance came to a quick stop at the closest curb, and soon two emergency medical technicians appeared with a portable gurney and a large metal container filled with supplies.

"What happened?" one of the EMTs asked.

They relieved Amanda and Hunter, and Hunter didn't waste a second before reporting on what had taken place. "We've got a fifty-year-old male who passed out while jogging. His name is Jack Howling. He went down approximately fifteen minutes ago. Ms. Dunlap started CPR within the first minute. We still don't have a natural pulse."

Amanda knew the faster CPR began, the higher the chances were of a patient surviving, and in this case Jack Howling's odds were outstanding. Yet he still wasn't responding, and that drove a surge of anxiety straight up her spine.

The EMTs hooked Jack up to a portable monitor, which showed a flat line. No heart activity except for when compressions were made. They delivered an electrical shock, causing Jack's body to jump, then waited. This time, the monitor showed the jagged shark-tooth rhythm of ventricular tachycardia. An airway was placed in his throat and an IV started while continuing CPR. They zapped him again, and after a long pause, an abnormally slow heart rhythm of thirty beats a minute—sinus bradycardia—appeared. Amanda's hopes soared at the sight. They placed him on the gurney and rolled him to the ambulance.

Amanda realized she'd wrapped her arms around Hunter and that he held her close. But she needed to be leader and calm the students down, so she broke away.

"How's everyone doing?" she asked.

Heads shook, and worried lines were etched across everyone's brows. Many were dumbstruck, others chattered nonstop, repeating all the events leading up to Jack's collapse.

Hunter closed the distance. He stroked her back and rubbed her burning shoulders. It felt good to have him near.

Dreaded thoughts of feeling responsible for harming one of her patients made her mute. But not Hunter.

"We may have saved someone's life today," he said, addressing the students, reframing the dramatic event and turning it into a teaching opportunity. "If you've never taken a class on CPR, I suggest you sign up for one." He glanced at Amanda.

"We'll be covering CPR in week six," she said, almost inaudibly.

"Week six. Good."

"Just before graduation," she said, already thinking that if she got the opportunity to teach another group she'd see to it they went over CPR the very first week.

Wendy ran back from the ambulance with bright red cheeks and an excited expression. "Jack's coming around."

They all rushed to the curb, and just before the ambulance door shut, the EMT gave the A-OK sign, which made a spring of relief trickle throughout Amanda's tense body.

Everyone, including Hunter and Amanda, cheered, and suddenly tears leaked from the corners of Mandy's eyes. Hunter cupped her face. With a look of pure empathy, he smiled and said, "You did good." Even Sophie squealed and kicked her legs from her stroller.

"Thank you," she said. "*We* did good."

"Knock it off." Back in the office that afternoon, Hunter chided Mandy for trying to take responsibility for Jack Howling's heart attack.

"What do you know about failure, Hunter? You've never washed out at anything you've ever done."

"That's baloney and you know it, Mandy."

"Name one thing you've ever screwed up at."

He approached and stared darkly into her eyes. "Us."

Her lids twitched when she realized she'd led him into forbidden territory. "I mean professionally."

"I was sent to boarding school from the time I was eight. My high school was strictly college prep. Failure was not an option. Look, we've been through this before. No one ever expected me to mess up. That doesn't mean I didn't."

"Name one professional thing that you screwed up."

"I wasn't the least bit interested in my dad's health. If I'd watched over him, made sure he'd seen his doctor more regularly, maybe he wouldn't have had a stroke and died."

"I'm sorry, but that wasn't your fault. Your father always kept you at a distance. You finally gave in and let him."

"You've probably got a point there, but it doesn't make me feel any better."

"At least your parents prepared you to go to university." She'd told him a million times how her parents had completely overprotected her. How they'd thought she should be working as a salesgirl at a department store. They had had so little confidence in her academic capabilities. She'd been so psyched out about her abilities that she hadn't even been able to qualify for university without going to the local community college first. "I felt so insecure that I had to give myself pep talks every day during nursing school, telling myself I was as good and as qualified as everyone else. Do you have any idea what it's like to be doubted every step of your life?"

"Then quit doubting yourself." He shook his head, fighting a strong desire to hold her in his arms and reassure her for the thousandth time that she was a natural-born nurse. "Mandy, you're a nurse practitioner. Shouldn't the last laugh be on them?"

"All my doubts came flooding back today. Suddenly I thought, What am I doing, taking these people's lives in my hands? They aren't just subjects in a study. I care about them." She shivered and he wrapped her in his arms. "I never thought anyone would go down in front of us like that. I know the odds are high—some of these people are high-risk for an MI—but I want to *help* them, *not* make them worse. They're not just names with numbers. They mean something to me."

"Jack never complained about anything," Hunter said. "He said he didn't feel any chest pain before he went down. You know damn well that sometimes it happens that way."

He'd just gotten off the phone with L.A. Mercy Hospital, where their patient had undergone an emergency angiogram only to discover one hundred percent blockage in a major artery and sixty percent in another. A stent would be of no use. Soon he would be rolled into the OR for a bypass graft.

"If that had happened when he was jogging alone, he'd be dead now, so quit kicking yourself," Hunter said.

"But how could we miss it in our EKG tests?"

They'd gotten out his twelve-lead EKG and twenty-four-hour halter monitor strips and searched for signs of Jack's condition.

Hunter shrugged. "Some really fit people compensate so well for their clogged arteries that they don't have symptoms. Has he ever complained about any chest tightness or feeling odd?"

Mandy shook her head. "Maybe he was covering for himself?"

"Or was in total denial. Either way, he fooled us." Hunter stood behind Mandy's chair and put his hands on her shoulders to rub away the obvious tension. She didn't protest.

"We need to make sure that every one of these participants reports *any* unusual symptom immediately to us," she said.

"Agreed."

"I thought we'd gone over that." She wove her fingers through her hair and took a deep breath. "I'll have to report this data under risk factors."

"It's a good thing everyone signed a disclaimer."

"Jack was such a fit guy I practically had to twist his arm to sign the consent."

"What made him change his mind?"

"He couldn't participate in the program without signing it. I think deep down he knew something was going on with his heart. It's just a hunch, but you know…"

"Yeah. Us guys hate to admit to our mortality. My father was a perfect case in point. He denied he had blood pressure problems until he had a massive stroke. His denial killed him."

"What about you, Hunter? Are you hiding anything?"

He laughed at the absurdity. "No more than you are," he said, and wondered why a peculiar expression suddenly covered Mandy's face.

That evening, Amanda stopped what she was doing at the sound of Hunter's voice. At her bedroom desk, she turned her swivel chair to face him and watched his shadow in the hall. He looked hesitant to enter.

She motioned him closer. When he didn't readily respond, she said, "Come *in!*" saying "in" as though it had twenty n's.

Hunter ventured into her room, scanning every corner with a sweep of his eyes. It made her a tiny bit nervous. "This is nice," he said. He sat on the edge of her bed and bounced a little on the mattress. "Nice."

"Is that what you wanted to tell me?"

A playful chagrined look changed his handsome face to almost boyish. "No. I thought we should throw some ideas around for Monday's Mending Hearts Club session."

"You must be reading my mind. Here's what I think." Amanda leaned forward, resting her elbows on her knees, lacing her fingers. She'd been contemplating nonstop the morning's dramatic events, and how to smooth things out with the other students. "We need to skip PT on Monday and call everyone together for a debriefing session," she said. "Maybe I can bring Social Services in for stress counseling if anyone wants it."

"Sounds like a plan," Hunter agreed.

"And maybe we can give them statistics on the odds of this incident repeating itself. Do you know any stats?"

He hopped up from her bed and pointed to her computer. "Not offhand, but I can find some."

They switched places, and she hovered over Hunter's shoulder while his fingers clicked and clacked across her computer keyboard. She wasn't trying to notice, but his hair smelled great.

Her legs wired with excess energy, she paced. "And we'll give them an update on Jack's condition," she said. "Do you think he's out of surgery yet? Maybe we should call again." She bit at a fingernail.

"Mandy, they said they'll be in touch. And the fact that he was in such good physical condition will make all the difference in the world with his recovery. That's what we need to emphasize. He almost died. We saved him. And once they fix him up, his prognosis will be outstanding."

"Maybe he'll agree to come back and talk to the class when he's out of the hospital—so everyone can see how well he's bounced back," she said, chewing on another nagging hangnail.

"I don't see why not. The way Jack likes to be the center of attention, I'm sure he'd do that."

She stopped pacing and grabbed her forehead. "Oh, God, Hunter. I told everyone right off that the program was meant to help them *avoid* invasive procedures like angioplasty, but in Jack Howling's case it would have detected his blockage without this trauma."

"No doctor would have ordered an angiogram for Jack according to his heart studies. He had no symptoms. His stress tests were stellar. Maybe if we routinely did echocardiograms after the stress test portion of this program, we would have caught it, but that's not how health maintenance organizations work. So quit trying to find ways to guilt yourself."

She paced in deep thought. "Maybe we should do that for future classes. That is if I get the opportunity and the funding. What if everyone in the group demands an angiogram now?"

"Will you quit worrying? We'll tell them exactly what they'll be in for, show them a film on the procedure, and most of them will reconsider. And if that doesn't change their minds, the sky-high cost of elective angiograms will. Trust me—no one wants to go through it unless it's completely necessary."

Amanda thought about the procedure, so similar to the one she'd need to go through to correct her Wolff-Parkinson-White syndrome, and fought back a shudder. She had several reasons for not wanting the procedure. Could she in good faith recommend it to others?

"I bet Noreen would get one," she said. Noreen was the thirty-five-year-old class hypochondriac, who'd signed on with the Mending Hearts Club without having any of the risk factors for coronary artery disease.

Hunter chuckled. "You may be right about that." He turned to face her. "This program you've created is going to change lives. You're doing a great service for these patients. Now, for the last time, quit knocking yourself."

The phone rang. She rushed to her bedside table and scooped it up before he could say another word.

"Hello?" she said. The heart surgeon was on the line. "Yes… Uh-huh… I see… Oh, that's great! Thank you for calling."

She hung up the phone and gave a relieved smile. "He did great! They wound up doing a triple bypass once they got inside. See? Even the angiogram didn't show all the blockage!"

Hunter clapped his hands and beamed back. Amanda tugged the air and let out a hoot. Without thinking, she ran toward him and jumped into his arms. He caught her, and she threw her arms around his neck, wrapped her legs around his hips. He spun her around in a circle and grinned while she continued to cheer.

The backs of his knees must have met with the bed mid-spin, and he lost balance. The next thing she knew, they'd fallen onto her mattress, with his back down and her straddling his hips.

# CHAPTER SEVEN

AMANDA looked down into Hunter's eyes and found them darkened with desire. He held her hips tightly in place over his, and neither of them dared to breathe. She watched his throat lift and roll with a swallow.

"I guess we got carried away," she apologized. He lightened his hold and she backed off from him.

Hunter catapulted off the bed as if it was a trampoline. "Well, it *was* great news." His intense gaze darted away from her face.

The sudden change in his demeanor both relieved and confused her. "This has been such a crazy day. I hope I can fall asleep."

Oh, that was a mistake. She could clearly read his mind, and his obvious ideas for helping her relax and go to sleep. They stood awkwardly for a few tension-escalating moments, considering the unspoken solution. She'd learned since their divorce that she couldn't handle casual sex. Besides, sex with Hunter could never be casual. Bottom line—neither of them had changed enough to venture into a deeper relationship, and, like it or not, sex would force them closer together.

Nah. Not going to happen. Why mess with the careful balance they'd worked so hard to keep while living together?

Hunter quietly cleared his throat. "A nice long bath might help," he said as he headed toward the door.

She scratched her cheek, where warmth had started to blossom. "Yeah, that's a great idea," she said, toeing the carpet.

"And I'll take a cold shower," he mumbled.

"What's that?"

"I said good night," he lied.

She'd heard him perfectly well.

Realizing it was Friday night, and he'd soon be packed up and safely on the road for home, a familiar empty hole returned to the pit of her stomach.

Hunter almost left the room, but stopped. "I've been thinking…instead of going home tonight, Sophie and I might stick around. Then tomorrow we can go to Mercy Hospital to check up on Jack. What do you think?"

Hunter's earnest support and his presence lifted her spirits more than she cared to admit. "I'd really like that."

Once he closed the door, she grabbed her robe off the bed and headed for the bathroom. She turned on the water spigots.

Even with her going to great lengths to avoid Hunter at every turn, they'd found their way back into each other's arms. How many times, since they'd started living together, had she stopped herself from slipping into old routines? It seemed so easy. After the initial shock of having him living in her home—with a baby, no less!—they'd learned to live civilly. But underneath every encounter, their old sexual connection thrummed. Lately it felt more like a beating drum.

She'd jumped into his arms and thrown her legs around his waist. What had she been thinking? Obviously she hadn't thought at all. When they'd been married, she'd done it all the time. Good news? Jump into his arms. Make love. Laugh. Love more. Work hard. Love more. Dream. Make love. That had been their well-rehearsed routine—until her dreams had clashed with his expectations. It had hurt like hell when he wouldn't fight to keep her. Why hadn't he?

Amanda suspected she knew the reason—because his parents had never fought for him, and he didn't know any different—but she wasn't ready to accept it. They'd dumped Hunter and Jade into boarding schools and kept them at a distance all their young lives until it was time to send them out into the world. How could he learn to completely open up with anyone when he'd never been shown how? And couldn't he ask the same question? Why hadn't she fought harder to stay with him?

With her body still tingling from being so close to Hunter, she slid into the tub. Subtle pulsations clouded her thoughts. One absurd thought popped into her mind: was it really so out of the question to have sex with her ex-husband?

Saturday morning, Amanda wore her favorite sundress, put on extra makeup and curled her hair. The look Hunter gave her when he first saw her was worth all the extra effort.

They packed up Sophie and headed forty miles south to Los Angeles, and Mercy Hospital.

"Mandy, if you don't mind, I'd like to stop on the sixth floor to see one of my patients. Mrs. Peters is having surgery on Monday, and I wanted to say hello and review her chart."

"Sure. I'll watch Sophie. Send me a text message when you're ready to meet in the cardiac unit."

"It may be a while. Her biopsy and thyroid scan confirmed papillary adenocarcinoma, and she's still in shock."

Amanda knew that, of the four main types of thyroid cancer, this was the most manageable. Yet she could totally understand being panicked over getting diagnosed with any kind of cancer and losing such a vital gland as your thyroid.

"Take all the time you need."

While they waited, Amanda took Sophie on a tour of the hospital maternity ward, where she could see other babies through a long window. But Sophie didn't seem too interested in the pink and blue blankets, so Amanda took her to the cafeteria where they shared some yogurt. Glancing around the room, she realized that people probably thought Sophie belonged to her. She sighed. Maybe someday.

They were halfway through their treat when a text message arrived from Hunter. She wiped Sophie's mouth and headed for the elevators to meet Hunter.

Jack Howling had already been moved from ICU to the step-down unit in the cardiac wing by the time she and Hunter stopped by for a visit. The pregnant ward clerk, obviously anxious to practice her mothering skills, offered to watch the baby while they paid Jack a visit.

He sat up in bed, looking pale but sturdy. His silver-dusted blond hair looked grayer than Amanda remembered. He wore the hospital gown backward, with loud flannel boxer shorts, and his chest was bandaged down the sternum with thick white pads and adhesive tape. Evidence of dried blood had been outlined with a pen on the top pad, to help the nurses assess the amount of oozing that continued from the surgical incision.

Only the surgeon was allowed to make the first dressing change. After that the nurses would do the daily bandaging honors. A chest tube containing bright red blood drained into a bedside container. An IV and piggyback bag infused into one of his arms, and another smaller dressing covered the incision in his right leg, where they'd stripped the veins to use for the bypass grafts.

Regardless of the daunting change in his life plans in the last twenty-four hours, Jack Howling seemed happy to see Amanda and Hunter.

"Don't get up," Hunter teased as they walked into the semi-private room. Another patient slept quietly in the adjacent bed.

"Hey!" Jack said. "Can you believe this?"

"If I hadn't seen it with my own eyes, no," Amanda answered, and patted his arm when she sat at the bedside.

"They told me I passed out yesterday."

Both Hunter and Amanda nodded.

"I swear to God I didn't feel anything was wrong."

Amanda wanted to kiss him for relieving her concern over being the cause of his collapse.

"And here's the real kicker—I didn't even have a heart attack. The nurses said it was the blockage that made me go down."

"No heart attack? That's fantastic," Amanda said. Without any damaged heart tissue, his prognosis for a full recovery was superb. "How's the pain?"

"The nurses are taking good care of me, giving me shots. I'm doing okay. But don't get me wrong." He placed his hand gingerly over his chest dressing. "I feel like someone ripped my chest open, chewed on my heart and sewed me up with chicken wire."

"That's an image I'd rather forget, thanks," Hunter said in a droll tone.

Realizing that wasn't far off from what had actually occurred, Amanda decided to change the subject. "First day post-op they should be getting you up and taking you for a walk."

"My nurse already warned me about that for later." Jack gave an affable smile. "You'd think they'd cut us heart surgery patients some slack."

"It's amazing how fast they get you guys up and around. I bet, barring any problems, you'll be home in less than a week," Amanda said.

Jack nodded, in quiet thought. Who would be at home to take care of him? she wondered.

"Hey, be sure to tell everyone I'm fine. I didn't mean to scare anyone."

"You put a few gray hairs on my head, but I think we'll all be fine," Amanda said. "Listen, Jack, when you get out of the hospital and feel up to it, I hope you'll come and visit the Mending Hearts Club."

"I'm already planning on it. I've got some unfinished business there."

Amanda's mind shifted to an attractive silver-haired widow in the group. So her hunch had been right. There was something going on. "Would you like us to tell Wendy she can come and visit?"

"Maybe wait a couple of days until I'm looking a little better?" Only one day post-op, and Jack Howling's vanity and potential social life had already taken the reins again. And that was an excellent sign.

Hunter had noticed subtle changes in Amanda over the past couple of weeks. She'd stopped wearing her gray sweats around the house. Her eyes didn't dart away the minute they caught each other's gaze. They'd started joking with each other again. And, just like old times, she'd jumped into his arms yesterday when they'd gotten the good news about Jack. But nothing spoke more clearly of her lightening up than when she took his hand on their way to the car, and her out-of-the-blue announcement on the drive home from Mercy Hospital.

"While you were seeing Mrs. Peters, I called Urgent Care and cancelled for tonight. I thought, since you guys are sticking around, I'd make a special dinner for us. Maybe we could rent a movie? How does that sound?"

He almost ran a stop sign.

"I think that's a great plan," he said, surprised, trying to sound casual. What had come over Mandy? Feeling reckless, he pushed his luck. "Any chance you're planning to make your blackened chicken?"

"Maybe." She beamed. "If you promise to make your famous apple crumble."

"I can work with that." Finding it hard to tear his gaze away, he glanced over his shoulder at his niece. "What do you say, Sophie? You want some of Uncle Hunter's apple filling?" The baby grinned and banged on her car seat, not having a clue what everyone seemed so happy about.

They made a quick stop at his house for more clean clothes, and another stop at the market, before heading back to Serena Vista. Two hours later, dinner was ready to be served.

Maybe it was because of their hospital visit that morning, or because it was a warm summer evening, but Hunter preferred to think that Mandy had worn the simple yet sexy sundress all day just for him. She'd even put on makeup, and the clear blue of her eyes seemed to glow from beneath her delicate brown brows. What he'd give to run his thumb along her neck and sample the fine silky skin.

She caught him staring in deep thought, and knowing her, she'd read his mind, so he looked away, as if the timer on the oven had just gone off.

It had. But he had to glance back when he noticed the quizzical glimmer in her eyes, and the way she twisted and chewed on her lips, as if holding back a question.

"What?" he asked, using pot holders to take the dessert out of the oven.

"I guess I'm still not used to your nose."

He rubbed the small, misshapen bump on the bridge self-consciously.

"Are you going to tell me?"

"I was chased by a wild pack of pachyderms."

"Give me a break," she said, and she threw an extra pot holder at him.

"It was for a worthy cause."

"You're telling me you broke your nose for charity?"

He chuckled. "Not exactly."

"Sooner or later I'm going to find out."

He managed to get her to drop the subject by uncorking a bottle of chilled white wine, and she followed him to the table as if he were the Pied Piper.

An hour later, they'd finished off the bottle, and he was clearing the dishes from the table.

Mandy stood in the kitchen at the sink, filling it with water. She glanced over the bar counter and smiled when he entered with an armload of dishes. He smiled back, realizing how often lately they'd gotten stuck in these goofy grin sessions. Maybe a shared bottle of wine accounted for this one.

Sophie chose the moment to let her general protest be known with a screech. Mandy rushed over, making the full hem of her dress twirl, showing off her long, athletic legs.

He lifted his brows and, stepping up to the sink, ran cold water over his hands.

"I think she's ready for bed," Mandy said. "I'll do the honors if you clean up. Deal?"

"Deal," he said, watching her sweep his niece up from her high chair and give her a hug and kiss. Sophie beamed with pleasure under the added attention, and yanked on Mandy's hair. She'd left it down for a change. He loved how the sepia waves cupped her shoulders and curtained her long ivory neck. It made him want to lift the hair and kiss the delicate skin of her throat.

Forcing his eyes away, he focused on the dirty dishes. But when Amanda brought Sophie into the kitchen, he feasted on

Mandy's good looks up close. She touched his shoulder as she passed to give Sophie a quick cleanup at the sink. Stepping aside, he tore at a piece of bread roll he'd found lying on the counter, suddenly ravenous and desperate for distraction.

"Thanks for making dessert. I can't wait to have some," she said.

"No problem," he replied, stuffing more roll into his mouth to keep from saying more.

She held up the baby for him to kiss, and it occurred to him that he liked this ritual of playing house and saying good-night to his niece. Wait! What had he just thought? He *liked* playing house? Being the dad and Mandy being the mom? When had that happened? It had to be the wine messing with his head. And besides, Mandy was safely back on her career track.

On her way through the living room, Mandy bent down and swooped up one of Sophie's toys. She glanced briefly over her shoulder as she did. Their eyes connected again, sending a pressing message through his spine. His sudden concern about his "little family" thoughts flew right out of his head.

Mandy knew how she affected him. He dropped the fork he was holding into the sink with a loud clink, and drew a breath through his teeth. She knew exactly what she was doing as she sashayed down the hall. Hell, if he'd known his famous apple crumble would make her flirt with him, he'd have made it a long time ago.

By the time she came back, he'd dished out the warm dessert and added a small scoop of vanilla-bean ice cream. Waiting on the counter was another bottle of chilled wine—just in case.

She smiled and inhaled when he handed over her bowl. "It smells great," she said, eyes closed, with an almost orgasmic look on her face. He knew from experience he could make her do better than that.

"Wait until you taste it," he said, barely able to control himself but grabbing his own bowl. They both headed for the living room, pretending the air wasn't thick with desire and potential.

Her ears perked up. "I notice you've put on some mood music." She glanced playfully at him before taking a bite of her dessert. Her gratifying smile almost toppled the last of his restraint.

"Music to eat by." He shoved in a huge mouthful to distract himself. Damn, the apple crumble *was* good.

A quiet jazz saxophone strung lilting notes together in a necklace of seductive riffs, and his mind kept wandering to the most inappropriate places.

Mandy was the one to carry away their dishes and return with a bottle of water, the second bottle of wine and two glasses. "Truth serum," she said, with a clear agenda in her eyes.

Just when he'd started to trust her, he suddenly felt on the spot. She wasn't interested in getting close physically; she wanted to talk. To probe. To delve. To force him to say things he never wanted to reveal. Just like old times. Damn, he needed a drink.

She poured and handed him a glass of wine, then opened the bottle of water and poured it for herself. "You told me your dad died, but you haven't said a word about him since. You feel like talking about him?"

He took a drink and licked his lips. "Not really."

"Come on, Hunt. Let's really talk for a change."

For the last month they'd both gone out of their way to keep things distant and casual, even while living together. Now, just because she wanted to, they should talk? Why the sudden change?

In defense, he wanted to throw her off course, and blurted the first thought in his mind. "Only if you tell me if you still plan on being Super Mom, and how you intend to make it all happen."

Mandy's eyebrows disappeared beneath her newly trimmed bangs.

She stared at the carpet, considering her life choices. She'd been over them a million times, but Hunter had brought it up again. She was twenty-nine, and if she really did want a big family, she'd have to get cracking on finding a man. The problem was if she intended to get her PhD in nursing, she'd be living her usual *vida loca*—of work, school and no social life—which would leave little opportunity for meeting someone. She sighed and took a sip of her water.

"I still want children, if that's what you're asking." She ran a fingertip around the rim of her glass and decided to be direct with Hunter. "And, judging from the way you've been taking care of your niece, you had nothing to be afraid of when I told you I wanted to be a mom."

"We had an agreement, Mandy. Our goals in life were as important as our love. You changed the rules—"

*Mid-game.* She finished his sentence. But their marriage hadn't been a game; it had been a promise that neither of them had fulfilled. If she'd been the true love of his life he'd have done anything for her. And even though she'd thought he *was* her one true love, she hadn't been willing to bend on that one major topic. So who was to blame? Both of them?

He took another drink. "I'm a professional. I can't exactly quit my job and change my lifestyle for a child. Neither can you."

"You've already done a version of that, and you're really great at it." Couldn't he see that?

"I'm taking care of Sophie out of obligation. Nothing more. I owe it to my sister and her baby to do a good job. That's as far as it goes."

"You could have fooled me."

Looking agitated, he took another quick drink. "How do you intend to be a mom and get your PhD at the same time?"

She looked away and shook her head. "It's not something I need to work out just now, but I've always said where there's a will there's a way. And kids feel the love no matter what—when it's genuine."

"I didn't."

She knew exactly what he referred to. "But that doesn't have to be the case with your own kids."

"Not going to have any, remember?"

She wanted to dig her fingers into her hair and scream. Why couldn't he see what a wonderful job he'd done, taking care of Sophie? Was there nothing that could change his heart?

The bitterness both he and Jade felt over their father clearly extended to their mother. Had Rhonda Phillips had to endure the loss of her husband alone? "Did you see your father before he died?"

Hunter shook his head and studied his glass. "Nope. The stroke was too sudden."

"What about your mother?"

"Saw her at the funeral. She'd already scheduled a lecture tour in Europe for the following month. I guess she didn't schedule grief into her plans."

Had Hunter scheduled grief into *his* plans?

Amanda knew from experience what she was up against with Hunter and his estranged parents. There was no love lost there, and it had turned Hunter against ever wanting a family.

She'd foolishly broached the subject back when they were married…when she'd missed her period. It had knocked the world and all her aspirations sideways. A feeling she'd never let herself experience before had swept up from her soul and embraced her so thoroughly she'd hardly been able to breathe. She wanted a baby. And more. She couldn't bear to do to one child what her parents had done to her as an only, lonely preemie. No. She'd have a full house, with noise and chaos, love and laughter.

Then she got her period.

But her dream hadn't changed. When she'd shared it with Hunter, he'd been horrified and would have no part of it.

"But you're not pregnant," he'd kept repeating.

"That's not the point," she'd tried to explain.

That day their true colors had shown, in a faint and disappointing palette.

Once she'd fully realized her desire to be a mother, and after their marriage had been tested and had failed, there had been no going back.

She had gathered her courage and faced Hunter, leveled her ultimatum. "Either we agree to have children one day, or I have to leave."

In a painful blow to her love for him, he'd let her walk away.

She finished her water and poured a splash more wine, then took a long draw. Tonight wasn't the time to bring this topic up. They weren't married anymore. But as a friend—and in a cautious sense she felt they'd become friends again—she wanted to encourage him to talk about his recent loss.

"I'm sorry about your father, Hunter."

But instead of answering, he chewed on his lower lip and stared sullenly at the carpet.

So far the "truth serum" hadn't worked. Especially on her. She'd kept all her deepest thoughts buried inside, unwilling to dig up old arguments. The moments yawned on, and Amanda desperately needed to change the mood. There was no point in rehashing their past. Their marriage was through.

"I've got to go to the bathroom," she said, rising on unsteady legs with wine tickling around her brain. Thanks to her, their relaxed and pleasant evening had plummeted into darkness. It was up to her to change it back. "And change the damn music while I'm gone. I want something with bounce."

When she returned, Hunter had done what he'd been told. He'd also drained his glass and was in the midst of pouring himself another one before topping hers up. A sign she'd really gotten to him. There was still a chance to undo the morose atmosphere.

She swooped by the couch to grab two pillows, then hauled off and hit him on both sides of the head. "I demand to know how you broke your nose!" she teased.

Brightening, he shot his hands up to defend himself. A Cheshire cat smile replaced the sullen face from before she'd left the room. He braced her wrists with his grip.

She managed to squirm one hand free, and kept on hitting him with the other pillow. "Tell me!"

He gritted his teeth. "Never." He played along, making the pillow fight all the more exciting.

She laughed with each swat she delivered.

"I'm gonna have to take desperate measures if you don't stop that," he said. *"Ouch. Hey!"* He picked up a pillow and thumped her back.

The crazy, wine-infused, childish behavior had unleashed something inside her. She giggled and wiggled her hips, taunting and teasing like she used to with him, a pillow in hand, ready to strike again. He looked excited and turned on.

After yesterday's close encounter with Hunter, maybe this was exactly what she needed, too. "I dare ya, mister." *Thump, whomp.* She landed two more good blows to his chest and squealed with pleasure, showboating like a professional football player after a touchdown.

"You little tease." He grinned and got up off the couch. "Now, *that's* the Mandy I remember."

He chased her around the table and walloped her on the butt when he caught up, then threw his pillow aside before grabbing her. He seized both of her wrists and dragged her onto the couch, laughing like a recently released madman. "Ha-*haaaa!*"

She struggled with all her might, but he was too strong. He pinned her arms above her head and leaned over her chest. The roughhousing had intoxicated her, and excitement surged in her chest as heat from Hunter's hovering body enveloped her.

"You owe me an apology," he said, huffing for air.

She squirmed her hips and kicked her legs. He mounted her thighs, forcing them down, keeping her in place beneath him.

"Heck, for a little whack with a pillow?"

He tightened his grasp.

"You owe me an explanation." Defiant, she taunted him, bucking her hips, refusing to cooperate. "How'd you break your nose?"

The sparks had turned to flames in his powerful Burnt siena eyes. He leaned into her and whispered in her ear. "I got decked by one of my patients."

His hot breath stunned her, and ignited her neck with sensation. Prickles shot out in all directions across her chest. Her nipples pebbled. She saw him study her breasts before raising his hooded eyes to hers. Heat traveled the path of his stare like lasers cutting deep into her senses. She looked away, for fear of revealing her feral desire for him.

She shook her head back and forth, denying the moment and the need. "Why?"

Before she could say more, his hot mouth landed a ragged, hard kiss on her lips. She saw it coming, yet didn't move out of his way. She kissed him back, just as eager. Their tongues met and lunged at each other. The kiss felt wet and wild and sexy as hell. Her body jolted to life and itched with longing. She caught herself in mid-reaction, throbbing between her thighs, damp, almost ready to let him have his way. She kicked her feet, twisted her hips and shook her head. No! She tore her mouth away from his, suddenly scared as hell to make love to him again.

"I don't know if this is such a good idea," she said, sounding as though she had just run ten miles.

He stopped the kiss, but didn't let go of her arms. His eyes burned with passion, wild and dark. "Then you shouldn't play with fire," he said, his voice raspy and challenging.

Amanda felt as though she'd been singed by a backdraft. She had never felt more alive in her life from the danger. Deathly afraid of giving her heart and body to Hunter again, she took refuge in sarcasm. "Give a man a good meal and see what happens?"

"This isn't about food, sweetheart." He sounded bold, but subtly loosened his grip and let her up. She missed the feel of him immediately.

Completely confused with herself, and almost timid, she was afraid to spark a new fire. But curiosity won out. "Why'd you get in a fight with a patient?"

He sat back on his knees and gave her a calculating glance. "I didn't say I got in a fight. I said one of my patients decked me."

"What for?"

"Doesn't matter."

She tugged on his shirt. "Yes, it does."

"I told a thirty-year-old father of two he had testicular cancer."

"And he decked you?"

"He didn't like the diagnosis."

"Did you press charges?"

"The guy had cancer!"

She extracted herself from his grasp and rose up onto her

elbows. Of course he wouldn't press charges. Hunter would never do that.

"How's he doing?"

"He's still alive and fighting."

"That's good. Did he ever apologize?"

Hunter grinned, showing the row of gorgeous teeth that she hadn't seen nearly enough since they'd started working together. "Several times."

She stared into his darkening eyes and saw the same longing she felt down to her toes. Her breath grew shallow with the realization that she'd encouraged this seduction, and wanted it just as much as Hunter.

He stood and reached for her hands, his dusky eyes probing her. She took hold, and with Hunter walking backward, followed him down the hall.

Just outside her room, Amanda reached for Hunter's neck. He swept her up by the waist. A whirlwind of movement followed as they intertwined arms and legs and lips.

His mouth took control, mapping a warm, moist orbit around her lips, pressing and pulling back, diving in and almost disengaging, but never losing contact. His tongue explored her mouth, thrilling and delighting her. God, she'd missed his taste. For every kiss he offered she kissed him back, hungry and eager for his attention. Her body buzzed so thoroughly with excitement she felt her skin vibrate. He must feel it, too.

His hands traveled over her bare arms, caressing and kneading the flesh. His palms felt hot, and she wanted him to touch her everywhere. She worked her own hands under his shirt, tested the expanse of his chest and shoulders. Solid. Smooth. She inhaled his scent and burrowed into the warmth of him.

Moans and sighs escaped their throats as they tortured each

other with long, hot kisses. Hunter reached beneath and raised her skirt to the waist, igniting a fireball of heat in her core. He discovered the barely covered flesh and sampled eager helpings of her bottom. Then and only then did he break from their kiss to inspect his surprise encounter with almost bare skin.

"Yes," she assured him. "It's a thong." Amanda blew the phrase out on a breeze of breath against his cheek.

He panted, and squeezed his hands tighter on each side of her hips, obviously pleased with her answer. Then he dove back in for another body-tingling kiss. He spread the wealth of his wondrous mouth down the side of her neck, kissing and nuzzling her skin, keeping the waterfall of sensations flowing. His hands lifted and massaged everywhere they touched.

A cascade of chills found every secret spot of her body, leaving her electrified and wet—a fantastically heady combination.

"I've waited all day to see you with your dress above your waist." Hot, breathy words brushed over her ear, tickling, taunting. "Do you have any idea how hot you are?"

She shuddered with pleasure and wrapped one leg around his thigh, pulling him closer. "No. Tell me."

He pressed into her hips, murmuring incoherent compliments…a sexy thesaurus of words that made her giddy.

He growled with pleasure while his thumbs slipped under the waist of the thong and worked the elastic down over her hips. She gave her full cooperation. In return, her hands, tense with anticipation, shot to his zipper. She caressed the heat and length of him through his jeans, catching her breath and nibbling on her lower lip in a futile attempt at slowing things down.

He held his breath. Carefully, she opened his fly and reached inside to the smooth and firm skin. He froze, and a guttural moan escaped his lips. Thrilled by the sound, she explored the warm flesh with gentle fingertips, held his width and felt him throb.

Energized with desire, and with him imprinted on her palm, she longed to trace him with her tongue. Heat washed over her body and pulsed in her core. She started to drop to her knees.

He groaned again, stopped her mid-drop and backed away.

Her euphoria was replaced by confusion. "Did I do something wrong?"

Hunter held her by the shoulders, stared deeply into her eyes with a feral gaze, and whispered fast and hard into her ear. "If you do that…I'm a dead man." He glanced over his shoulder. "You have no idea how much I want to make love to you, but what about Sophie?"

She giggled at his absurd and sudden concern. "You are such a *dad*."

His eyes widened at the realization. They grew serious and stared at each other for a few seconds. She could only imagine the battling thoughts of denial running through his mind.

But right now she wanted to get him back on track. "Okay. Take me here. Take me in my bedroom. Take me anywhere… just take me."

# CHAPTER EIGHT

"I've missed you, Mandy." Hunter joined her on the bed and gently kissed her forehead. His lips wended their way across her eyes and cheeks, and finally over her mouth.

Amanda felt his warm breath as he stopped and looked with love-softened eyes straight into her heart. "I've missed you, too."

"Are you sure you want to do this?" he asked.

As crazy as it seemed, she wanted more than anything to be in this moment with Hunter, to pretend that now was all there was and there would be no consequences tomorrow.

She would have debated more about the aftereffects, but Hunter kissed her long and thoroughly, and she felt it all the way down to her toes. All thoughts vanished from her mind as she grew nearer to the moment and the need. She wrapped her arms around his neck and drew him closer. Heat flared between them—surely he felt it, too? His arms tightened around her. Their kiss became more urgent, feeding the flames already coursing through her body. She squirmed and twisted his shirt in her fists to keep him close.

He pulled the shirt over his head and quickly did the same with her dress. A cool breeze marked the loss. His chest was firm and broad, and lightly dusted with dark hair, and she remembered every muscle and curve. His hand caressed one breast through her bra, while his mouth found the other. Chills sent Amanda spinning with a symphony of sensation. Hungry for his touch, she moved her hips and he pressed down onto her with his own. She savored his weight, pulling him closer, harder against her body, wanting more. And more.

Frustrated at the barrier between them, she rubbed her hand over the denim-clad bulge in his pants. "Take them off," she gasped.

As though reluctant to leave her breast, he kissed and suckled one last time, sending a jolt to her belly. He rose up onto his knees to remove his already unzipped jeans, and she helped him slide them down his legs. He was clearly desperate for her, and his penetrating caramel eyes never left her face.

Alone. Finally together again. She could hardly believe what was happening as she reached for his jaw and caressed it to make sure he was real. His intense stare erased any doubt.

Frantic to be together, they didn't waste time with any further preamble. He sheathed himself with a condom and entered her quickly. She gasped at the surge of sensation, then relaxed and welcomed the length of him into her warmth, savoring the fullness. They mated in a nearly forgotten primitive dance of intense, luxurious sensation and hard, frantic rhythm. He clenched his jaw, drove deeper into her, stoking the fire.

Sensing his hunger, she groaned her approval and encouraged his every move. She bucked her hips, begging for satisfaction. He worked to please her, not having forgotten what she liked. She coiled tighter, drawing him deeper and deeper with each silken stroke. She throbbed with his powerful thrusts, alert and riveted to the sensation of Hunter deep inside. He held her firmly in place, paralyzing her with pleasure.

Amanda gasped with near unbearable sensation, and heard him groan as they grew ever closer to the brink. He found her perfect spot, filled her completely, and she could barely hold back another second. As though reading her mind, and every inch of her body, Hunter made her thunder and writhe with spasms both overwhelming and exhausting. And finally, when the overload of sensations began to settle down, he let himself go, stirring her up all over again.

A vague memory worked its way up from the thick soup in Hunter's head. A deliciously warm body lay next to him in the golden early-morning light. Mandy. He snuggled in close and inhaled the scent of her hair. About to nibble her shoulder, he stopped short when he heard Sophie's cry. How long had he been out of it? And how long had Sophie been crying?

He hopped out of bed and pulled on his jeans as Mandy stirred and looked sleepily over her shoulder at him.

She heard the cries, too.

"Oh," she said. "Can I help?"

"Nah. I've got her." He dashed out of Mandy's room to the other female in his life.

Sophie sat in her crib, looking more disheveled than Mandy, with wispy hair sticking to her drool-dampened cheeks. Yet she smiled when she saw him, and he couldn't help but do the same. When had he fallen for her?

The thought of having kids had scared the hell out of him back when he was married. But now, with Sophie, he'd discovered a secret serenity, and he admitted he liked taking care of her. But the responsibility felt monumental at times, and a month of hard work was so much more doable than a lifetime commitment. Although he had to admit that Sophie brought far more pleasure than pain.

Remembering Mandy's statement in the hall before they'd made love, he winced. *"You're such a dad."* Those words had almost made him lose his erection! Yet here he was, walking the walk. Hell, maybe he *could* handle being a dad? Nah, it took a hell of a lot more than changing diapers.

On autopilot, he lifted Sophie out of the crib, kissed her gooey cheek and put her on the makeshift changing table. He studied the sticky kid carefully and succumbed to a shudder. Nope. He wasn't going down the daddy road. No way.

A shadow appeared from behind him, and Sophie's face lit up.

"Hi, sweet pea," Mandy said to the baby. "Want me to get a bottle for her?"

"That'd be great," he said, acting as though they hadn't just had the most mind-blowing sex since their honeymoon and—well, just about every day after that when they'd been married.

She'd put on a short Asian-style robe, giving him lots of leg to appreciate. He smiled and recalled her honey-warm skin next to his. It hadn't been a dream.

Sophie kicked him in the stomach and grabbed a fistful of his arm hair. He flinched and his gaze shot back toward his niece, who was now innocently playing with her toes. He managed to deal with the task at hand—a filled diaper and a hungry baby.

Sophie gave him a sloppy raspberry.

"Yeah. Back at ya, kid." He shook his head and grinned. Contentment took root in his heart.

As if he'd almost slid into a trap, he caught himself and tensed. As far as kids were concerned, he still preferred to keep parenthood a foreign word.

"Guess who you get to see today," he said. Today was Sunday, the day Jade could have visitors before being released, and he'd promised to bring Sophie with him. "Momma. Can you say Mom-mah?"

Back in a flash, Mandy handed the bottle to Sophie just as Hunter connected the last snap on her cotton pajamas.

"May I?" Mandy asked, when Hunter had lifted his niece.

"Sure," he said, handing the baby over to her.

She gave her requisite wide-eyed, goofy-grin greeting, which Sophie never grew tired of, and carried the baby to the living room.

Mandy settled in an overstuffed chair and fed the bottle to Sophie, casually running soothing fingers through the child's hair, looking as natural as any mother. He'd noticed that fact all too often over the last few weeks. Right this minute Hunter stopped to enjoy the sight, but instead of relaxing, he felt tension knot in his chest. *Don't get her hopes up. She drew a line in the sand three years ago and you haven't changed your mind.*

How could he have forgotten that important part of the equation when he'd decided he wanted to win her back? He'd been thinking with his other brain again.

For less than a heartbeat, all of his well-thought-out reasons for never wanting a family escaped him. What if? he wondered. He caught himself, scratched his head and started for the kitchen. "I'll make some decaf."

With a distant, oblivious, motherly gaze, Mandy said, "Sounds good."

But it wasn't good. He'd just made love to his ex-wife and now he wanted more. She'd never be completely his again… unless he changed. And could he trust that she wouldn't pull another switcheroo on him?

An inkling of the night before filtered back into Amanda's brain. Had it been a dream, or had she actually done what she thought? She remembered seeing Hunter over her, under her…beside her. Oh, God. Her cheeks grew hot with the memory.

They might have had one incredible night together, but Amanda knew instinctively that that was as far as they could go. "Friends with benefits" wasn't her style.

She could try to pretend there was no harm in sleeping with Hunter, but Amanda wouldn't buy the rationalization. Been there, done that. It hurt. Time to move on.

She watched him in the kitchen, making coffee, and brick by brick she began to rebuild the wall that needed to stand between them. By the time the coffee was ready, and he'd brought her a cup exactly the way she liked it, her fortress was complete.

They didn't speak another word about what had happened between them Saturday night—as though they both knew it had been a mistake and were being extra careful not to repeat it.

Hunter dashed off with Sophie for Jade's visit, and Amanda spent her Sunday as she always did, routine being her best friend and her survival plan.

On the Monday of their fifth week of cohabitation, thankful she had daily data from the Mending Hearts Club to input, Amanda worked diligently on the computer in her room.

Somehow she and Hunter had managed to work together on the project without letting on that anything had changed in their relationship. Erring on the side of safety, Amanda decided to pick up more shifts in the Urgent Care clinic, in one last futile attempt to avoid him and keep things less complicated.

The news came that Jade was to be discharged from her in-patient treatment program, and Hunter was ecstatic…until he realized he'd no longer have a reason to live with Mandy.

When he told her, Mandy was genuinely happy for Jade, but Hunter thought he saw disappointment at the back of her deep-sea eyes. Maybe he was projecting his own feelings.

"When will she be home?" Mandy asked.

"Tomorrow night."

She chewed on her bottom lip, and instinctively he grasped her arms and looked closer at her.

"Anything wrong?" he asked, unsure if the gleam in her eyes was happiness or an early sign of tears.

"I'm thrilled for Sophie and Jade to be together again. The sweet pea deserves her mother." She looked away from him. "It's just that having the two of you living here has drummed up all sorts of mixed feelings."

"I know what you mean." It was time to admit to the truth. "I keep wishing we could go back and fix things."

She looked into his eyes with a steady, sincere gaze. "I didn't lie to you when we got married. I really was totally committed to my career. No one was more surprised than me when I went all maternal at the first sign of a missed period."

He tightened his grip, remembering to his horror how excited she'd been about possibly being pregnant. Immediately he'd questioned her ability to be both a professional and a mother, citing his own mother as evidence. He never wanted children because of what he and his sister had had to endure. In the end, that immovable stand had proved to be the key downfall of their marriage.

"You gave me an ultimatum because I didn't jump on the parenthood bandwagon. I had a knee-jerk reaction." He shook his head, seeing the demise of their marriage so much more clearly now. "That was exactly the way my father handled things all my life, without care for my feelings or thoughts. He'd just steamroller through with his decisions. You gave me no choice, as if you didn't care what any of it meant to me, and I couldn't live like that."

"I'm sorry, Hunter."

"So am I."

They studied the truth in each other's eyes for several moments.

Sophie didn't have a clue about their sincere confessions, or minutes on the clock, or waiting for her mother to come home. She shrieked, demanding their sudden and undivided attention. Bouncing up and down in her playpen, it was obvious she wanted to be lifted up and not ignored.

Obviously thankful for the distraction, and breaking from his hold, Mandy rushed over and reached for her. She let Sophie test out her legs by holding her hands and walking her around the living room. Soon the baby got brave. Mandy gently let go of one hand, but continued to walk with the child, who had one hand flapping in the air. As the baby's confidence and balance grew, Mandy let go of her other hand. To their amazement, at only just over ten months old, Sophie took two steps on her own before she realized she'd lost her support and plopped onto her bottom.

Mandy's eyes practically popped out of her head. Hunter couldn't believe what he'd just seen, either. Mandy clapped her hands and did a little happy dance, which tickled Sophie and changed Mandy's confused and on-the-verge-of-tears look to something much more ecstatic.

"She walked!" Mandy said, her eyes shining with excitement. Then her expression changed and her hand shot to her mouth. "I'm so sorry. I never expected her to walk. I didn't mean to…"

He reached for her arm. "It's okay, Mandy. You haven't stolen anything from my sister. It will be her baby's first step when Jade sees it, too."

Without any logical explanation, Mandy got teary-eyed, shrugged free from his grasp and briskly left the room.

Amanda threw herself onto her bed and let the tears roll. Damn she was going to miss them—her *pretend* family. If only things could be different.

Hunter thought exactly the same way she did when it came

to Jade and Sophie. He would no more dream of robbing Jade of witnessing any of her daughter's firsts than she would. His response just now had written volumes on her heart.

That was one more reason why she'd started to fall in love with Hunter again.

He tapped on her door. She quickly swiped away her tears and wiped her nose on a tissue. "Yes?"

"Can we talk?"

Oh, God. Could she handle this right now?

Without waiting for her response, he tentatively entered her room, holding Sophie on his hip. She loved how he looked carrying the baby.

With a solemn face, he edged closer. "I've been thinking how much living with you these past few weeks has meant to me, too. Sophie has blossomed under your care. And I'd almost forgotten how much I missed being around you."

"No, Hunter, she's blossomed under *your* care. You're a natural-born father. You just won't admit it yet."

He shook his head. "I seriously doubt that I'm father material. Somehow I just managed to get through this month without harming her." He grinned at Sophie and she swatted at his face. "But I couldn't have done it without you."

"That's what parenting is all about—sharing the duties and care of your children. That's what families do—support each other." She wanted to tell him that even though she'd dodged him and fought her feelings every step of the way, she'd never felt more complete in her life than during these last few weeks. But she couldn't allow herself to be any more vulnerable right now. So she bit back her true feelings and made an appropriate response. "I'm grateful I had the opportunity to help out. It's been great."

He came closer and reached for her. "It's been more than

great." He hugged her with his free hand and kissed her cheek. She grazed his lips with her own, her lashes fluttering with overwhelming feelings.

The baby squealed and lightened the mood. Thank heavens for Sophie. But Amanda couldn't hold back her tears. "I'm going to miss you so much, sweet pea."

As though knowing the seriousness of the moment, Sophie grew quiet and reached for Amanda's face. Mimicking what she'd just seen between Hunter and Amanda, she gently pressed her moist and soft mouth against Amanda's.

On Sunday afternoon, long, toned and tanned legs in shorts jogged ahead of him. Beneath a fluorescent-yellow sports bra, modest breasts, perfectly fit for Hunter's palm, lifted and dropped with each stride. Mandy.

Hunter had been to her house and found no one was home. He suspected Mandy had spent the morning working at her computer and needed to stretch her legs with a long run. That was what she'd used to do when they were together. Since he knew the route she always took, he'd gone out scouting. And here she was. She looked lonely. Hunter decided to keep her company.

He'd driven to Serena Vista because now that he no longer had his niece to take care of, he didn't know what else to do. There was so much he wanted to tell her. Good thing he'd come prepared, bringing water and wearing his jogging shoes. He parked his car, set off in a sprint, and tried to catch up with her.

"Hey!" he called. Mandy didn't respond. "Wait up!"

This time she must have recognized his voice, because she glanced over her shoulder. Her eyes grew bright with surprise. "What are you doing here?"

He finally reached her. "I just *happened* to be jogging in the neighborhood and *happened* to see you." He huffed out the bogus words, fighting back a giveaway grin. "Thought I'd keep you company."

She sputtered a laugh. "Right." But she didn't seem to mind him joining her.

Hunter settled in and matched Mandy's rhythm and pace, but as they strained side by side up a hill, his breathing soon grew ragged from the effort. He smelled fresh sweat, and something new—a hint of gardenia scent. Even jogging she smelled good.

"You're killing me," he gasped.

She smiled with lips outlined by minute beads of perspiration. "You invited yourself along, remember?"

Mandy could still outrun him, but today she slowed down to allow him to catch up. He dug deep inside and followed. At the top of the hill, he bent over, rested his hands on his knees and sucked air in and out of his lungs. He'd been spending all his time with the Mending Hearts Club walkers, and now wished he'd pushed himself and accompanied the joggers more often.

She ran in place while he recovered. "Lucky for you I have to cut it short today."

Determined not to be a wimp, he joined Mandy jogging in place, his breathing almost back to normal.

"Don't tell me you've got another shift at the Urgent Care?"

"Nope. But I'm at a crucial point in my journal article."

He took a swig from his water bottle. Mandy did the same.

"Maybe I can help you with that," he said.

"You ready?"

He nodded.

She flashed a mischievous smile his way before trotting downhill. The look had managed to take his breath away and left him longing for contact like a horny teenager. He tried to catch up with her and, mimicking an adolescent, took what was left in his water bottle and squirted it on her back. Mandy scrunched her shoulders and squealed.

"Oh, you'll pay for that." She ran a wide loop around him, opened her bottle, ran to his side and poured the remaining water over his head. She giggled before breaking into a sprint.

Hunter sprang ahead with renewed energy, grabbed a hold of her waist and yanked her off the sidewalk onto the grassy knoll. He lifted and whirled her around in a wide circle. She squawked and fought, lost her balance and fell into him. He held her tight against his chest in a damp embrace for one exhilarating moment.

"You have no idea how turned on I am right now," he whispered roughly into her hair as he held her in a bear hug. *Did I just say that? Damn right I did.*

Mandy threw her head back and laughed from her gut. Now he was glad he *had* said it. She squirmed and pushed with amazing strength on his chest, surprising him, and knocking him onto his ass on the grass.

"Then you'll have to catch me!" she said, and she sprinted for home.

Invigorated by hope, Hunter took off like an Olympian in the hundred-meter dash.

They raced home and barreled through her door. What else do you do after a run but shower? Together. With your ex-husband. Was she crazy?

An hour or two later, Amanda woke up lying on her tummy, mildly disoriented. She opened her eyes to find Hunter on his side, resting on his elbow, studying her face. They'd started making love in the shower and finished off in her bed. Feeling exquisitely relaxed, she must have fallen off to sleep.

"I had the most wonderful dream," she said with a smile. "You were in it."

He smiled, too, and ran the flat of his hand across her back. "I want to be in all of your dreams, Mandy."

His warm palm caused gooseflesh across her hips. She rose up on her elbows and searched for the clock. It was two in the afternoon.

He stroked his hot hand over her bottom, grabbed another condom and slowly, purposefully, rolled on top of her.

She felt the weight of him at the small of her back, hard and straight as he parted her legs and drew her up onto her knees. His breath warmed her ear, tickling chills down her neck. If she'd been capable of thinking, she might have questioned her sanity, but she was too far gone for that.

Within seconds, she had surrendered to the pleasure, burrowing her face into the pillow to muffle her gasps and cries. Hunter's breath fanned across her neck and shoulders, enveloping her in heat. His intimate groans fueled the wildfire in her body, causing every nerve ending to ignite.

Unrelenting, he pushed her over the threshold and into another long, luxurious free fall, only moments before he erupted with a growl.

They stayed wrapped in each other's arms for the rest of the afternoon. Dappled in early-evening shadows, Hunter started to speak.

"Yesterday I stayed up most of the night talking with Jade. She really seems to have her head straight now," Hunter said.

"That's great to hear." Amanda wove her fingers through his thick dark hair.

"She made me realize that I need to deal with my father's death. I guess I can't ignore it anymore."

"She's right."

He rolled onto his back and stared at the ceiling. "I've been thinking that as crazy as it sounds, even though I hated him all these years and never wanted to be like him, I still loved him. I just needed to know that he loved me, too."

Excited by his discovery, she rose up on one elbow and looked into his face. "I always knew that, Hunter. I'm glad Jade forced you to admit it."

His gaze shifted to her face. "After he died, my mother gave me a letter he'd written but never sent to me when I got accepted at med school. You'd think it would mean something to me, but I still can't bring myself to open it."

"Because you're afraid you won't be able to keep thinking of him as a monster if you find out how he really felt?"

"I've spent my whole life detesting him. Why change now?"

"Because it's important, Hunter. Your attitude has made a hole inside you. It's holding you back emotionally and you'll never be complete until you deal with it."

The expression on his face changed from tense to defensive. He rolled onto his side to face her straight on. "And how do you know all of this? You're still trying to impress *your* parents."

Trying to keep things from escalating, she gave a gentle laugh. "I think I've moved beyond trying to impress them. Now I'm doing everything to impress the world."

"Whatever." He backed off. "You've come a long way, and you're still the most impressive woman I've ever met. Maybe it's time you gave yourself some credit."

He reached out to hug her, but before she could relax, she wanted to get the last and most important truth off her chest.

"I have to be honest with you. Being around Sophie has made my desire to have babies stronger than ever." She drew her head back in order to look into his eyes. "If you can't give me a family, there's no point in us moving forward."

His gaze didn't waver. "And I have to be honest with you, too. I owe you that. I'm scared witless I'll suck at being a dad and screw up some innocent little kid's life." He let go of her and shoved his hand through his hair. "I can't commit to that."

"But you've already proved otherwise with Sophie." She reached for him and held him close, anchoring her head to his chest. "You're not your father, Hunter. You'll never be like him."

He kissed her cheek with soft warm lips, and she prayed that, between she and Jade, someday they'd force him to see the truth.

"No. I'm not my father," he whispered.

"Read the letter, Hunter. Go home and read it with an open heart and mind." She lifted her head. "And one more thing…"

His gaze took its time reaching hers, and disappointment colored the usual deep brown tint of his eyes. He'd tensed, and with all her heart she wished she could say something other than what needed to be said.

"Until you've dealt with your true feelings about your father and mother, and can say you're open to being married *with* a family, there's no point in us seeing each other."

He squinted, looking confused and wounded.

"The sex is great, Hunter, but the price is too high."

# CHAPTER NINE

HUNTER rolled off the bed and dressed before he looked at Amanda again. "Why is it that every time I start to trust you, you hit me with a curveball?"

He searched her eyes. She jutted her chin and stood her ground, knowing how overwhelming her request had been.

"I'm being honest, Hunt. We'd only wind up in the exact same situation again, and we know how *that* worked out."

After several moments of strained silence, he made a thoughtful retreat, and although Amanda's heart felt like a rock and her legs like gelatin, she threw on her robe and showed him out.

He stopped on the doorstep, reached for her and traced her jaw with his thumb, as if imprinting her face in his memory. She detected a slight tremor. God, would it come to that? They'd be nothing more than faint memories in the course of each other's lives?

"Don't give up on me yet."

The phrase lightened her love-wary heart and injected it with cautious hope.

The final week of the Mending Hearts Club thankfully whizzed by, though every day, when Amanda saw the pensive and reticent

Hunter in the office or classroom, her heart squeezed in her chest. Would today be the day when he'd announce he'd come to his senses? But he never spoke about it, and every afternoon ended in disappointment, though she tried her best to keep her chin up.

He'd reverted to following her original misguided rules of careful etiquette, yet he maintained a deep and caring attitude with their patients. They both made a point to avoid direct eye contact. She feared that all her personal dreams for them were finally lost, since he never broached the subject of where they stood again.

At least she'd achieved her goal with her career. The class had proceeded without further incident, and everyone was set to graduate with a ceremony.

Jack Howling made a special appearance. The group was thrilled to see him, and for someone who'd undergone heart surgery only weeks before he looked great.

"Have I got stories to tell." He grinned and paced at the front of the class. "Anyone want to see my scar?"

The group laughed, but he was serious. He quickly unbuttoned his loud Hawaiian shirt with pride, and displayed the long wide scar down the center of his chest. Amanda noticed a few Mending Hearts Club participants' eyes bulge. The scar was a sobering sight.

"The thing is, I was in denial. I've always been a fit guy, and when I started feeling 'different,' I just chalked it up to aging. I thought if I pushed myself harder, I'd get past it. I came to Mending Hearts because I saw a flyer at my doctor's office. Yeah, my cholesterol was kind of high, but I was on medicine for that. And sometimes my blood pressure went up for no good reason. But I looked good, and for the most part felt great. Yet a little voice told me to join up. Nurse Dunlap and Dr. Phillips saved my life the morning I collapsed. And now, with three fresh veins feeding blood to my heart, I'm a new and improved man."

He grinned at a particularly rapt listener in the front row. Wendy.

"And the best part of all about coming to the Mending Hearts Club is I met my future wife."

The attractive widow blushed and covered her face. Amanda noticed the huge rock on her hand. Wow.

"I know it's quick, but when you almost die you realize you've got to grab life by the tail and hold on for a great ride."

Why couldn't she and Hunter have that attitude?

During Jack's amusing remarks, Amanda gazed around the room. The "suits" from Mercy Hospital were in attendance, and Dr. Hersh, the medical director, had arrived, along with some people from Hospital Administration.

Though she'd told her parents about today's event, she hadn't officially invited them, and she wasn't surprised when she didn't see them. Amidst all that was going on, one important message about her parents had forced its way into her mind. *We didn't know any better.* How many times had they claimed that excuse? She hadn't minced words when she told them exactly what she thought of their withholding her childhood heart condition from her. And they had reiterated by saying exactly how they had felt about Amanda's endorsement of the angiogram that had harmed Chloe's kidneys. How could they claim to love her if they kept secrets from her?

The thought of withholding information made her think about Hunter as she walked to the podium.

He still wasn't here.

Her heart slid to her stomach.

Amanda smoothed her skirt, cleared her throat, and had prepared to speak when the double doors of the auditorium swung wide. A colorful baby stroller was pushed through, and a striking and healthy-looking Jade Phillips was behind it. Sophie sat regally inside, emitting a squeal and beaming a smile. Amanda couldn't help but grin back. The backs of her eyes stung. Several heads turned and grinned, and Amanda realized she hadn't been the only one to miss the little Mending Hearts Club mascot.

Hunter stepped from behind the doors, carefully closing them. He glanced up with a look of chagrin, realizing he'd disrupted the program. "I'm sorry," he said. "Don't mind us, Mandy. Please go on."

Hunter stood dutifully at the back of the room, hands in pockets, looking more handsome than ever in brown pants and a tailored tan silk shirt outlining his fine physique. With his chin raised in pride, he seemed as glad as Amanda to see such a good turnout. Maybe it was well-earned pride at what they'd accomplished. Together.

They'd maintained a pristine work veneer even over their resurrected rough-edged relationship. She'd reiterated her desire to be a mom and he was still leery. Some things never seemed to change. If nothing else, Amanda had learned she could survive anything where Hunter was concerned. At least she would always have her career.

She glanced at him in the back of the room, and the tiny unhealed wound in her heart ached. It would take a lifetime to completely get over him.

Amanda coughed and cleared her throat to get everyone's attention. Once the chatter had settled down, she worked to find her voice.

"Six weeks ago, Dr. Phillips and I met twenty patients in dire need of shaping up their heart health. Today, nineteen of you will be the first to graduate from the Mending Hearts

Club program, and a twentieth will receive an honorary certificate of completion." She nodded toward Jack Howling, who smiled back.

"Over the last six weeks, through hard work, dietary changes and exercise, we've seen a collective four-hundred-point drop in total cholesterol, a two-hundred-and-fifty-point drop in triglycerides, a one-hundred-and-forty-point increase in HDL, and a two-hundred-point decrease in LDL. Every single participant now has a cholesterol ratio within normal limits."

The crowd, made up of hospital bigwigs, Mending Hearts Club students, family and friends, applauded.

"The average blood pressure has decreased by ten points, and resting heart rates have dropped by seven beats per minute. We've collectively lost a hundred pounds!"

More applause.

"But the most important statistic is one that cannot be measured, for it will last a lifetime. One hundred percent of you report that you generally feel better and have more energy than when you began this program. And your lab results reflect that change. Again, through everyone's hard work, along with Dr. Phillips and my efforts on your behalf, we have learned positive behavior modification which will benefit each and every one of you in every aspect of your lives. I sincerely hope these new habits are ingrained in your hearts and minds as you prepare to leave here today, and that you will maintain your new vigor for the rest of your lives. Now it's up to you."

Amanda took her time gazing across the auditorium. So many faces, both familiar and strange, smiled back. This was the moment she'd dreamed about since she'd earned her master's degree—a time when her efforts would prove her capabilities.

"I'd like to think we've all been given a second chance for a fresh start in life, and I can only hope none of us wastes it. If you'll each step forward when I call your name, Dr. Phillips will hand out your certificates."

At the sound of his name, Hunter rushed forward and joined her at the podium. His presence, and the soon-to-be absence of it, wrapped her in a veil of longing. She handed him the computer-printed certificates. He gave an encouraging smile, and she tensed when their fingers brushed. Static electricity ran up her arm. Amanda read out the first name to distract herself.

An hour later, after a reception of punch, low-fat cookies and fruit gelatin, the first graduates of the Mending Hearts Club had all gone home. And Amanda had been given the best news of her life. Mercy Hospital, knowing how cost-effective preventive medicine was, had agreed to sponsor her program for their health maintenance organization patients at all three California Mercy hospitals—and she would be the facilitator.

One of her professional dreams had come true! She'd created, formed and hatched the program, then brought it to fruition…with the help of Hunter.

The only thing left was the finishing touch to her medical journal article and Hunter's official seal of approval. The next step would be earning her PhD. Nothing could stop her now.

Taking to heart Hunter's jibes about her "life is work" attitude, she'd tried to lighten up over the past six weeks—except it had backfired where Hunter was concerned. He'd taught her that being less strict with her diet wasn't the end of the world, that a night off from work for a movie was time well spent, and that laughter was always the best medicine. Hell, hadn't she been the one to start their pillow fight? She was far from being incapable of change.

And, since there was no time like the present, she gathered her confidence and searched him out. Snaking through the guests, she found Hunter and tugged on his sleeve.

His eyes brightened when he turned to find her there. Amanda gave Jade a hug and Sophie a kiss. The happy response from both was genuine.

"You look wonderful," she said to Jade.

"And so do you," Jade answered, showing no hint of depression.

"Hi, sweet pea. I've missed you."

Sophie's legs pumped and kicked with excitement.

"Oh, wait," Jade said. "Watch this." She put Sophie down and helped her gain her balance. With Jade barely holding on to one finger, the baby took several steps. Jade beamed her pride, then let go, and Sophie took the next three steps all by herself. "She just started walking last week!" The grin on Jade's face was close to the greatest gift Amanda had ever been given.

"That's so wonderful."

Hunter smiled benevolently at her. It was the first time in over a week that he'd looked her in the eyes for more than a heartbeat. Their little secret about Sophie's first steps would always be safe.

The grandmother of the Mending Hearts Club rushed over and applauded Sophie's feat, then introduced herself to Jade, flipped out her grandchildren's pictures, and began an animated conversation. Seizing the opportunity, Amanda turned to Hunter with a flutter of butterflies in her stomach.

"I saved a special bottle of champagne for today. I know things have been kind of stiff between us for the past couple of weeks, but I think we deserve to celebrate after all the hard work we've done. You feel like helping me celebrate?"

The pleased gaze of his molasses-colored eyes was all the answer she needed.

\* \* \*

Hunter wasn't going to kid himself. Mandy had suggested a picnic, most likely to avoid being alone with him in her house. She didn't trust him to keep his hands off her. Could he blame her?

Instead, they had agreed to meet and dine under the stars on the hillside of the Serena Vista Presidential Library. From there they had a sweeping view of the surrounding hills and mountains, where several communities were tucked into the winding expanse of the valley floor. In the distance, hundreds and thousands of lights sparkled like an intricate diamond necklace across the hills. A warm summer breeze playfully lifted Mandy's hair as she served their dinner from deli containers onto paper plates.

Hunter smiled when she handed him a pink plastic flute of champagne.

"This time it's my turn to make the toast," she said.

Savoring her uncomplicated beauty, he nodded. He watched for nuances in her expressions, searching for clues about her feelings for him, but failed to read past her smile. She'd told him point-blank what he'd need to do to win her back. At least she'd been up-front about it this time.

She stood proudly, the victor of her professional dream.

He lifted his glass as she began.

"To dreams. To health. To never giving up. To hero mentors with nieces full of life." She tossed him a playful glance. "And, finally, to our success."

They clicked and drained their glasses, and Mandy quickly refilled them.

Maybe it was the open sky, or the balmy end-of-summer night. Maybe it was sharing this special moment with the lady he wanted more than anything else in the world. But Hunter felt compelled to share the truth about his dad's letter with her.

She'd told him to read it. From now on he wanted to share everything with Mandy.

"I read my father's letter."

She stopped mid-sip, interest blooming in her eyes.

"He said I made him prouder than anything he'd ever done for himself when I decided to go to medical school and got accepted. He realized how he'd failed me as a father. Even apologized." Hunter scratched the back of his neck and pondered on how different things could have been. "You were right, Mandy. In his own messed-up way he loved me. He just had a lousy way of showing it.

"After he died, when my mother found and gave me the letter, I asked her why he'd never given it to me. She said her hunch was he'd been ashamed. She admitted she'd talked him into giving me something practical. As I recall, it was a check for a few thousand dollars. Like a fool, he listened to her. How could he think money was more important than telling me he loved me?"

Mandy caressed his cheek and peered into his eyes with what could only be described as a look of empathy. Not love.

He couldn't bear to think of Mandy pitying him, so pulled away and finished his drink in one swallow. Since he'd skipped lunch, the fizzy bubbles went directly to his head, and Mandy's soft features and delicate skin became a temptation he found too hard to resist.

"Will you dance with me?" he asked.

When she slowly nodded, he was surprised and extremely pleased. But what about music?

He pulled out his iPod, chose a slow dance and put an earphone into one of each of their ears. Then he pressed Play. The music swelled seductively when he took her into his arms as though this was exactly where she belonged. He slowly guided her around the grass in the evening light.

A soulful male voice sang an old classic about love. No one invaded their privacy. Tonight the hillside and the heavens were all theirs. Mandy held her champagne flute in one hand and shared sips with him as they slowly danced forehead to chin, round and round. His hands rested comfortably at the small of her back. A perfect fit.

"You mentioned today that everyone had been given a second chance?" he said.

She smiled and nodded, though her eyes were closed and her mind was obviously distracted by the lush music. The smell of night-blooming jasmine, the soft caress of an early-September breeze, the tart and tantalizing taste of champagne—all things he was acutely aware of, and he imagined she felt them, too. But for him there was something more. Surely she knew how precious she was to him?

"Mandy, I've been thinking."

A smile stretched across her glistening lips.

"I'd like you to give me a second chance."

Her eyes popped open. They stopped dancing. The serene expression that had covered her face the prior second changed to one filled with questions. He felt her tense in his arms.

"The thing is, before I never totally let you into my life. I set boundaries we couldn't cross, and when you changed our plans and mentioned children, I freaked out. All the pain I felt as a child came rushing back, and I couldn't bear the thought of hurting a kid of my own."

Her eyebrows lifted at his explanation.

"Okay, so Jade told me that part. But you were right. Having Sophie around added so much to my life. Sharing her with you brought me greater happiness than I ever thought possible. What I'm trying to say is I realize I'm not my father. You'd never let me get away with being like that. I'm—"

Amanda put her fingers against Hunter's lips to stop him
om saying another word. Three years ago this speech was
hat she'd longed to hear. She'd prayed he'd come around to
er way of looking at things. Now, after living with Hunter and
ophie, and especially since they'd moved out, she, too, had
ome to realize the importance of putting a child first. Maybe
at knowledge was the key to why she'd spent her whole life
ying to prove herself good enough to her parents…and the
orld. If only she could accept herself.

*Take a chance. He deserves to know. Open your mouth
nd tell him.*

The truth stuck in her throat.

If he knew about her heart condition, he'd treat her as if she
ere fragile, and quite possibly use it as an excuse to stop her
om fulfilling her big dream. It might give him the excuse to
sist again that career and family didn't balance out, and force
er to make a choice. They both already knew how that scenario
ad worked out.

Old pain from the knowledge that she hadn't changed nearly
s much as she'd hoped tore at the corners of her mind. The
ast thing she wanted to do was battle her demons tonight. Not
n the night of her victory.

"Hunter, for tonight let's not talk about the past or the
uture. Let's just be in the moment. Right here. Right now. Just
ance with me."

But he'd brought up a subject she couldn't drop from her
nind. He'd once told her she wasn't ready to care for a baby,
nd he had been right when he'd chastised her all those years
go. *"You couldn't care for a houseplant, let alone a child."* He
adn't had any more confidence in her then than her parents.
Maybe he had been right. Then.

How could she put a child first when working full-time and

going to school while wholeheartedly pursuing her career? Livin
with Sophie had shown her how time-consuming and demand
ing a baby could be. Who would pay the price for her academ
pursuits? An innocent child? She'd finally seen the light.

Determined to see things out, she'd made some min
changes in her plans. Now she'd rearranged her dreams to g
full speed ahead with her education and then, once she'
obtained her PhD, settle down to begin the life and the famil
she'd always longed for. But could Hunter wait that long? An
could he accept her as she was?

Everything had changed when she'd been diagnosed wit
Wolff-Parkinson-White syndrome. Now she didn't even kno
if her heart could handle a pregnancy. The fanciful famil
dream had seemed so unlikely until recently that she'd neve
thought to ask her doctor about childbearing.

Hunter deserved to know about her medical condition *an*
her big secret—that she'd fallen in love with him again. But sh
wasn't ready to open her heart and tell him the writing on he
soul just yet. Not before she had her plans worked out. Unt
then, she couldn't take the risk.

"Let's just dance," she repeated, forcing her mind to focu
away from all the thoughts twirling inside her head to the musi
and the night…and Hunter.

On her doorstep, Amanda gently kissed a severely perplexe
Hunter goodbye. "I promise to sort things out. We'll talk… soon

What would it be like not to see him every day now that th
Mending Hearts Club was over? She missed him already.

"If you really mean what you said, maybe we can test th
waters for getting back together."

"I've never been more serious, Mandy."

Judging by the sincere glint in his eyes, she believed every word. So why wasn't she rushing into his arms and telling him she loved him?

Because she hadn't been honest with Hunter.

"I hope you'll understand that I need more time to think this through."

"It's been three years, Mandy. What's a few more days?" he said with a rueful expression as he walked into the night.

Maybe after she'd worked everything out, she'd tell him about her heart condition.

First thing after arriving home, she walked to her bedroom and went online to look up PhD degrees in nursing that offered part-time programs. Maybe she could work part-time and go to school part-time and still manage to have a life...with Hunter? And if she couldn't risk a pregnancy herself, maybe they could adopt?

Dare she so much as think of the possibility?

Afraid to let her dreams take flight, she concentrated on the computer screen until she found what she was looking for. She'd lost track of time when an instant message popped up. It was from Hunter.

*Hi. Want to go for a run with me tomorrow morning?*

What was he up to? He'd offered his heart and she'd cut him off. He wasn't backing down. And running always helped clear her mind. He'd understood all her qualms tonight, promised her time and space to work things out, but obviously he had no intention of letting things lie. It was definitely time to cut the guy some slack.

*Sounds good to me.*

She wrote back, thankful he hadn't taken her kiss-off at the door the wrong way.

*I'll meet you at 9 o'clock. H.*
*I'll be here. Good night. A.*

Amanda printed out applications for two nearby schools that offered a part-time doctorate in nursing before she went to bed. If he was willing to bend, so could she.

But were they really meant to get back together?

Fear and doubt, like a wicked cold wind, blew through her tenuous confidence, sending her to bed with a chilled and heavy heart and keeping her awake most of the night.

As arranged, Hunter arrived on Mandy's doorstep at five minutes to nine on Saturday morning. She opened the door, squinting into the bright sun.

"Good morning," she said.

"Yes, it is." Would he ever get used to the impact she had on him? He took her in as a lazy smile spread across his face. Thanks to keeping a diet journal and eating better, she'd put a few pounds back on, and it looked great on her.

Their gazes locked and lingered as messages of wonder and lust jumped back and forth between them…at least on his side. He had no intention of letting her forget how much he wanted her.

"Let's go," she said, all business, closing the front door behind her.

They warmed up with a walk to the end of the block, before switching to a jog and finally running.

The sun soon baked the back of his neck, warming him to the point of sweating, and Mandy's expression changed to one

f concentration. She stretched out her steps and resembled a
azelle as they worked their way up a long incline.

"Have you done any more thinking about what I said last
ight?" he asked.

She glanced at him with a wild-doe look in her eyes.

"I'm sorry for pressing you, but I've figured a few things out
ince reading my father's letter. I never completely gave myself
) you when we were married because I didn't know any better.
And your parents never believed in you enough for you to trust
oving anyone who couldn't believe in you and your dreams."

Her eyes brightened, then subtly dimmed. "Did Jade tell you
) say that?"

He nodded guiltily.

"Do you know how many times I've asked myself why you
et me walk away?" she said.

The words stabbed like a knife. "Mandy, I'm sorry."

"Why didn't you fight for me?"

His failure at being the husband she'd deserved made him
vant to give up. But he wouldn't this time. He'd lay it all out
s honestly as he could. Even if the picture was an ugly one. "I
lidn't know how."

Tears glistened in her eyes, and she cast him an indefinable
glance as she dug in and ran harder.

At the top of the hill, she seemed to struggle, but she made
t. Okay, she didn't want to talk about it while they were run-
ing. He could understand that. Downhill was a breeze. But he
vouldn't let her avoid the topic today, as she'd done last night.
After the run, he'd press for a response.

Toward the end of the next block, her hand flew to her neck
o check her pulse.

Concerned, Hunter slowed down. "Are you all right?"

She stopped running, and seemed far more out of breath than

she normally would have been after such a short distance. "I. I need to go the ER." She could barely get the words out.

Apprehension rose up like a brick barrier and he slamme into it. "What's wrong?"

She was breathy and nervous, and her eyes grew wild as she was in panic mode. "Heartbeat. Too fast."

Hunter felt her pulse. Holy God! He could hardly count th beats. Surely it couldn't be that fast? Her skin felt cool, yet sh was sweating.

"I feel dizzy," she said, paling right before his eyes.

"Are you having chest pain?"

"No." She shook her head.

"Sit down. No! Lie down." For a medical professional, he' quickly unraveled into bumbling boyfriend. *Think!* "Bend you knees." Hunter slipped his cell phone from his pocket an dialed 911. "Try the Valsalva maneuver," he said, grasping a anything that might be remotely of benefit. Realizing he migh be making her more nervous than she must already be, h schooled his voice. "That will help your heart slow down."

He answered all the questions from the nine-eleven operato and dutifully waited. And prayed.

What in the hell was happening to Mandy?

He sat by her on the grass, holding her hand, all the whil watching every twitch of her face and every change in her ex pression. She was young and fit. This was a fluke. Surel nothing could be life-threatening? He felt her pulse again. was still thready, and over two hundred beats a minute. H couldn't believe it. Thankfully the rhythm wasn't irregular, a in atrial fibrillation, it was just ultrafast. Since the Valsalv maneuver hadn't worked, he rapidly rubbed over the vein in he neck, giving her a carotid artery massage in another attempt t slow down her pulse.

"Mandy, stay with me."

"I'm here."

He worried that her blood pressure would drop too low and she'd pass out. He elevated her legs by propping them on his shoulder, and didn't take his eyes off her until the ambulance arrived ten minutes later, along with a fire truck. The EMTs began their intake. Mandy's blood pressure was only eighty-five over forty while her heart rate remained alarmingly rapid. On the portable monitor, the rhythm looked like supraventricular tachycardia.

"You're going to be all right, sweetheart. Your heart is young and strong. They'll straighten this out in no time."

The oxygen helped her breathe easier. They started an IV to give her fluids to help bring up her blood pressure, and to give access in case she needed emergency drugs. They called ahead and warned the local hospital they were on their way.

Hunter rode in the back of the RA unit, fearing he might lose the woman he'd come to love all over again. He held her hands and bent close, looking into her eyes. Fear still occupied her gaze.

"Everything will be all right. They'll give you medicine to slow your heart. I won't let anything happen to you." He squeezed her cold hands tighter.

The hint of a smile crossed her lips. He glanced at the monitor. Her heart rate was unchanged.

A weak tap on his hand drew his attention back to the woman he loved. Her nostrils flared as she tried to catch her breath. He knew she wanted to tell him something, but she couldn't manage to utter a sound.

# CHAPTER TEN

THE EMTs rolled Amanda through the double doors at the back of the small ER at the local Serena Vista hospital. Ceilings and lights whirled past, making her squint. The blare of voices assaulted her ears and made her flinch. Though her heart galloped in her chest, and it was hard to catch her breath, she tried to relax in the knowledge that soon her condition would be treated and she'd be back to normal.

And Hunter was by her side. He'd finally told her everything she'd dreamed. He wanted a second chance and was open to her dreams. Hell, he'd stopped short of asking her to marry him again. But she'd withheld the biggest secret of all: her heart condition. She'd never meant for him to find out like this.

She was placed in a vacant room in front of the nurses' and doctors' station. Everywhere she looked people were crowded together, reaching over, bumping into and dancing around each other. Someone nearby had recently used a bedpan, and the institutional air freshener was doing a poor job of covering the odor.

The tiny emergency department had clearly outgrown itself. Outside the rooms, gurneys lined the walls, surrounded by drapes resembling shower curtains around a bathtub to accommodate extra patients. From her vantage point, every room and gurney in sight was filled.

She heard Hunter answering questions and discussing her with the attending doctor and nurse by the bedside. No, she didn't use drugs. No, she wasn't taking any type of weight-loss aid. No, to his knowledge she wasn't using any herbal supplements. *No, she didn't have any preexisting heart condition.*

She raised her hand to say something, but the nurse had hooked her up to a heart monitor and a blood pressure cuff. Her oxygen level was checked by pulse oximetry. They placed a nasal cannula inside her nostrils and weird-smelling air blew up her nose. Her heart rate registered two hundred and forty-eight beats per minute, and her realizing that made the rate increase a few beats more.

Amanda needed to tell the doctor about her Wolff-Parkinson-White condition, but Hunter was intently monopolizing the conversation.

A tall doctor named Rodriguez squinted and studied the heart monitor. "It almost looks like a circus movement tachycardia," he mumbled to himself. "Let's get an EKG. *Stat.*"

Five minutes later, two doctors were poring over the EKG. "The QRS interval is narrow. I'm not a cardiologist, but it looks like orthodromic conduction."

She could only pick up bits and pieces of their conversation over the racket from equipment being rolled into and out of the room, and the piercing voices competing with each other in the hallway. As the patient, she felt left out of the equation.

The black-haired Dr. Rodriguez appeared at her bedside and looked down at her with concern in his midnight-colored eyes. Hunter stood on the other side of the gurney. "Dr. Phillips tells me you're a nurse?"

She nodded.

"Your heart is in a tachydysrhythmia known as circus movement, and we need to break the cycle. We don't know why this has happened, but since you're having symptoms with this pre-excitation, we need to treat you." Dr. Rodriquez pointed toward her monitor unit. "As you can see, your blood pressure is quite low, and you're short of breath and dizzy, so we'll start with a calcium channel blocker and go from there. If necessary, we will cardiovert you chemically with Adenosine, and if that doesn't help we'll use direct current."

She tried to get a word in, but he kept on telling her how he intended to treat her heart problem. Amanda cursed herself for not buying the medical alert necklace her doctor had suggested when he'd first diagnosed her. But she'd been in total denial, and eventually had forgotten about it. Some educator she'd turned out to be.

She tried to catch her breath and say *Wolff-Parkinson-White,* but she kept getting cut off. If they chose the wrong treatment, or if they treated her for atrial fibrillation instead of WPW, they could make matters worse.

"Is there any chance you might be pregnant, Ms. Dunlap?" Dr. Rodriquez asked.

Her eyes darted to Hunter, who looked as surprised as she felt. She shook her head.

"I ask because Adenosine's safety for use during pregnancy hasn't been established."

"Give me the shock," she finally managed to say.

"But we may be able to slow down the heart rate with the drug."

*No.* She shook her head, knowing it was the more extreme of the two treatments, but was fail-safe. "The shock." She just wanted to get this over with so she could move on with her life. A new life she hoped to share with Hunter.

"The shock's safety during pregnancy is questionable, too." The doctor persisted in his one-note samba.

"Not pregnant. Shock me."

Hunter leaned forward. "Are you sure you want to go that route?"

"I've got Wolff-Parkinson-White syndrome," she said, though she had to take a couple breaths between words. "I need the shock."

Hunter's brows shot up, then furrowed. "Why didn't you tell me this—"

Dr. Rodriguez broke in. "Were you officially diagnosed?"

"Yes. Last year."

"In that case, I'll have a nurse give you a sedative and I'll call Anesthesiology to prepare you for electrical cardioversion. The nurse will have you sign a consent." Before Dr. Rodriquez left the room, he turned back. "If you know you have WPW then you should also know there is a way to fix it with cardiac ablation. You don't ever have to have one of these episodes again."

"I know," she said.

Hunter looked at her in total confusion. "Why haven't you taken care of this?"

She felt too exhausted to explain all her reasons for putting the procedure off. Number one being fear. Deep primal memories of being helpless and poked and probed, of feeling cold and alone in hospital after hospital as an infant and toddler, came to mind. And fear that she'd wind up like her twenty-one-year-old patient—dead on the table. Number two: denial. She'd spent enough time being a weakling as a child. She'd survived. She could handle this one last flaw if she monitored herself.

She could also throw in the fact that she'd weighed the odds of dealing with occasional bouts of SVT versus going through an invasive heart procedure and had erred on the side of conservative treatment. She'd even bargained with herself that if she taught other people to care for their hearts then maybe she'd be cut some slack on her own condition. That approach seemed the opposite of scientific, but hope and faith went beyond science.

Obviously nothing had panned out.

Fighting the machine gun rhythm in her chest, and Hunter's incredulous stare, she started to feel overwhelmed. Pins pricked behind her eyes and she bit her lip. Instead of giving in, she shut an emotional gate and clamped her jaw. She'd handle this in her own way. If he loved her, he'd understand.

Dr. Rodriguez started to usher Hunter out of the room as the anesthetist arrived. "Time for us to go."

Hunter quickly bent and kissed her forehead. "I'll be outside."

Knowing he'd be there comforted her, but she worried what he must think about her never mentioning her condition. The trust pendulum swung both ways.

An anesthetist wearing teal-colored scrubs and a flowery surgical cap leaned over the gurney and introduced herself. She had small green eyes that matched the scrubs, and she smiled while she placed large adhesive electrode patches over Amanda's chest and behind her back.

Not knowing that Amanda was a nurse, the anesthetist continued using layman's terms. "The electrical shock causes all the heart cells to contract simultaneously, and that split-second interruption allows the heart to regroup and return to its normal heartbeat." As the IV had been placed by the EMT before their drive in, the woman cleaned one of the access ports and said, "I'm going to inject a quick-acting sedative, and when you wake up you won't remember a thing."

Amanda knew that the electrical shock was painful, and welcomed the sedation. The procedure had left two large red marks on her chest and back last year. Feeling the effects of the medicine almost simultaneously as the nurse injected it,

Amanda's head began to swim. A quick thought sped past, about her world being like a roller-coaster ride with Hunter around, and how much more beautiful life was with him in it. She felt separated from her body, as though it was floating on a soft raft out to sea.

More quick notions danced on the horizon of her mind. Hunter's love was a gift. Drifting deeper and further away from consciousness, she held on to the thread of one last thought. If she loved him, she needed to trust that he'd accept her exactly the way she was.

And then there was nothing.

Hunter paced the crowded ER waiting room from end to end while Mandy was being cardioverted. He fished out his cell phone and walked outside, past the "No Cell Phones" sign on the other side of the hospital doors. Several other people were there, elbows bent, phone to ear, presumably explaining their loved ones' circumstances into their mobile devices.

Hunter dialed a number he hadn't realized he still remembered until right now. "Hello? Chloe? This is Hunter Phillips." *Your ex-son-in-law.* "I thought you'd want to know that Amanda is in the hospital. It's her heart…again."

Wolff-Parkinson-White? Why the hell hadn't she told him? He'd known she'd changed. His gut had warned him she'd been holding something back. No wonder she'd put herself on a cardiac care diet and was so passionate about the Mending Hearts Club. He'd been right, something *had* knocked her world sideways, but never in a million years would he have guessed what.

Sure, she'd done her best to cover it. Once he'd broken down her early barriers, she'd kept things aloof or playful whenever they got too close. Not that he hadn't enjoyed their carefree romps. And she'd been professional to a fault, kept him at an arm's distance. He'd made it past that hurdle, too. Once they'd made love, he'd thought it would all be smooth sailing—until she'd dropped the bomb with her final ultimatum.

And now she'd managed to astonish him again, with this surprise condition.

He'd finally opened up and shared his every thought with Mandy. He'd given opportunity after opportunity for her to do the same, only to find out she'd hoarded a huge secret.

How could she love him if she didn't trust him? Disappointment draped him like a heavy curtain. His shoulders drooped under the weight. Finishing his brief call with Amanda's mother, he switched off the phone and went back inside to the waiting room.

After several more minutes of pacing, he approached the middle-aged woman wearing a blue smock with a volunteer badge at the hospital front desk.

"Can you check how much longer before I can go back in to see Amanda Dunlap?"

The deeply creased woman, with youthful blond weaves throughout her graying hair, picked up the phone and dialed the emergency department ward clerk. "This is Janet at the front desk. I've got a Mr…" She looked up at Hunter.

"I'm Dr. Phillips. Amanda's ex-husband."

"I've got Ms. Dunlap's ex-husband here, a Dr. Phillips, and he's wondering when he can come back." She listened for a moment and replaced the receiver in the cradle. "They'll call you as soon as possible, Dr. Phillips."

Frustration had him gritting his teeth. The thought of Mandy going into complications sent his heart speeding. He couldn't bear to lose her now that he'd found her again. Even if he was no longer sure who the hell she was.

Here she was, running a preventive heart care program, when all along she was the one who needed to have her heart fixed. When had she been planning to tell him? And, more importantly, could he ever trust her again?

Hunter loved her and believed in her, but she had to be honest with him for their relationship to work.

Finally, after several more minutes, the blond volunteer waved him over and led him to the ER doors, where she punched in a code to open them. "She's in room five."

"Thank you."

He entered anxiously to find Mandy resting comfortably, though looking drowsy. He bent to kiss her forehead. She moaned. Once he'd established she was okay, his gaze shifted to the heart monitor. Normal sinus rhythm. Thankfully.

After a reassuring conversation with the ER doctor, he took one last look at Mandy and walked away. Until she could be completely honest with him, there was no point in proceeding with his plans.

What kind of man ran out on a woman in the ER, leaving her to go home to the parents who'd never thought she'd thrive? A man who needed more time to think.

He'd give her a few days to recover, and then because he loved her, he'd convince Mandy to have the heart procedure. In the meantime, as far as their relationship went, he'd demand nothing less than honesty—which meant she'd have to approach him. Right about now, the thought of waiting for her to see the light and come to him felt worse than open-heart surgery.

The last thing Amanda remembered at the hospital, besides the small green eyes of her anesthetist, was Hunter's shocked and hurt expression before he kissed her and left the room. Had that been before or after the procedure?

Her hand rose to her chest and gently massaged the tender spot on her skin. A loud purring noise alerted her to Jinx, nestled inside the crook of her other arm. She was home. "Hey, buddy."

How had she gotten here?

Still dazed, she stared at the bedroom ceiling, comforted by the slow and perfect rhythm of her heart. But it didn't last for long. A whooshing sound drew her attention to her bedside.

"I've brought you some herbal tea," her mother said. She set it on the nearby table and helped her sit up, then propped her with several pillows. These were the tender touches of someone who cared about her. Something she hadn't felt from her mother in ages.

"Mom? What are you doing here?" Her mother handed her the cup. She took it and sipped.

"Hunter called us. We rushed over to the ER as soon as we heard."

Amazed by her mother's sudden appearance and obvious concern, she glanced beyond Chloe's shoulder to find something more astounding. Her father. An expression of equal attentiveness softened his usually intense gray eyes.

"You had us worried, sweet pea," he said.

Putting on a cheery facade, she blew on her tea and said, "No worries. They fixed me." She took another sip.

Her father sat at the bottom of her bed and massaged her foot with a knobby hand. "Until the next time. You know you've got to be careful. Why were you out there running like an athlete?"

"Dad, nothing in particular sets this condition off. Stress, maybe. No one knows for sure. I could be sitting at my desk all day and have the same thing happen. Haven't we had this argument enough? I was born a preemie, but I'm a strong adult woman now. Jogging is good for me."

"Maybe you should tell your heart that," her mother mumbled.

Amanda felt her blood pressure rise as she handed the teacup back to her mother. Was this some cruel joke Hunter had played on her for not being honest? Okay, so she hadn't been straight with him about her condition, but she had it under control. She hadn't thought he needed to know because once he did, he'd treat her just as they did—like an invalid. She couldn't bear him treating her like that. And she really didn't need the aggravation of dealing with her parents right now.

"I'm going to take a nap, if you don't mind," she said.

Her mother kissed her forehead, the way she had each night as a child. Her father waited his turn and patted her hair.

"Sweet dreams, sweet pea," he said.

As aggravating and overprotective as they'd always been, she knew her parents loved her. What was it like for Hunter, never to have felt his parents' love?

Maybe it was time to cut her parents some slack. And if she was the changed woman she purported to be, she needed to say a few things to them.

"Mom and Dad?"

They both turned at her bedroom door.

"I want you to know I'm grateful you're here. And I love you. But someday you're going to have to quit trying to protect me. I'm a grown woman."

Her mother came back to her bed and sat tentatively. Her father sat down on the end of the bed and gave a rueful smile. "We love you, too."

"We'll be here when you wake up," her mother said.

There was so much more she needed to tell them. Most importantly that it was beyond time for them to accept her for who she was—a strong and capable woman. If they couldn't see that by now, they must both be wearing blinders. But somehow she could already sense a change in them, as if this attack had been a wake-up call to appreciate who their daughter really was.

Amanda snuggled back down into her pillows, wanting nothing more than to sleep. But her brain wouldn't let her push certain thoughts out of her mind.

She hadn't told Hunter about her condition because she couldn't trust how he'd respond. But after all he'd proved to her, *why* couldn't she trust him?

She thought about the ablation procedure she'd have to undergo to fix her heart and shuddered. A specially trained electrophysiologist would make an incision in her groin, similar to an angiogram, and introduce a wire, winding it all the way up to her heart. Her *heart!* Every step would be watched through fluoroscopy, with live images guiding the doctor's hands, but human error was unpredictable and in this instance could be deadly. Once they'd found the faulty heart tissue area, they'd sedate Amanda and actually try to make her heart go into irregular rhythm on purpose—the crux of her problem.

Wouldn't that be tempting fate? What if they couldn't turn it around? With all the experts and resources close at hand, Amanda should trust that she would be safe, but still the thought sent panic through her limbs. What if they couldn't stop the tachycardia? Or, worse yet, damaged cardiac tissue or peripheral nerves, and made her an invalid?

*Damn.* Why had she read the EPS consent so thoroughly? Especially the part that said "…and even loss of life." It was a wonder anyone signed it.

Once they'd found the damaged area, they'd cauterize it with radiofrequency ablation, cutting off the extra electrical pathway and solving her problem once and for all. Well, in ninety percent of the cases anyway. Was going through the invasive procedure, risking life and limb, worth the ten percent chance of failure?

So far she'd settled for the watching and waiting approach to dealing with WPW. Many people lived out their lives with the condition without any problems at all. But her heart condition had reared its ugly head too often, and had become a quality of life issue. The fear of another attack would always be hovering over her subconscious. She never wanted to experience what she'd gone through today again. Crossing her fingers and hoping to beat the odds was no longer good enough. And on top of everything else it was stupid.

Exhaustion swooped in, causing her to lay back her head and close her eyes. There was so much to think about. Most importantly, she wondered where Hunter was. When she needed him the most, he'd sent for her parents. But could she blame him?

Just before she drifted off to sleep, a quick memory passed before her eyes. She'd wanted to tell him that she loved him in the ambulance. What if she'd died without him ever knowing?

## CHAPTER ELEVEN

MONDAY morning, Amanda wore her best outfit for her doctor's appointment—a pale gray designer skirt and a periwinkle silk blouse to bring out her eyes. And she wore matching slinky shoes an inch higher than she preferred, making her feel too tall and even more nervous. But she was on a mission and she wanted to look just so. Nothing would stop her today. Hmm. Maybe she should undo the top button of her blouse.

Yesterday afternoon, when she'd woken up from her drug-induced nap, all her weird dreams about Hunter had finally made sense. She'd had an epiphany. Before, when they were married, she'd only fallen in love with Hunter with her heart and body. This time around, she'd fallen in love with her heart, mind, body *and* her soul. He'd become everything she'd ever dreamed of in a partner, and she couldn't imagine her life spent without him.

For weeks she'd kept him shut out from her deepest secret—even after he'd told her he wanted a second chance. No wonder he'd left her at the hospital and run off.

Just because she'd made up her mind about their future, it didn't mean he'd go along with the program. But unless she was honest with him about her feelings, she'd never find out.

A nervous quiver tensed her stomach.

One thing she'd learned beyond everything else in life was

that there were no guarantees. But rather than follow in her parents' negative low-expectation footsteps, she'd chosen to reach for the stars and be all that she could ever hope to become. Now living with and loving Hunter again were part of that dream. She just needed to convince him that she trusted him, and that she could be trusted to never keep another secret from him.

A short, plump nurse with a contagious smile stepped into the waiting room and called out her name. Amanda stood and followed her to the nurse's cubicle.

"My name is Maria," she said. "Since you're a last-minute add-on, we didn't get your chart delivered. What brings you to Mercy Hospital Clinic?"

"I need a referral to Cardiology," Amanda said.

"Any particular reason?"

"Dr. Phillips will understand," Amanda said with a coy smile. "But here's what I need you to do…"

Hunter hung up the phone, sat in his office and stared out the window, putting his headphones in place. He would listen to Mozart's "Rondo" from *Eine Kleine Nachtmusik* in an attempt to uplift his mood. Today was his first day back seeing patients at Mercy Medical Clinic since being assigned to the Serena Vista Clinic. He had a full schedule ahead of him, and was thankful to be busy. But in the meantime, he needed something to help get his day started. Mozart seemed to be the ticket. Later he'd need more music, to help get him through the first day of the rest of his life without Mandy.

He'd gotten to work much earlier that morning, no longer having to pack up and cart his niece around everywhere he went. Being honest, he missed Sophie—even felt a little empty without her. But the biggest gap in his heart came from losing the love of his life…again.

He felt a tap on his shoulder and turned to find his nurse Maria smiling with a mischievous twinkle in her eyes. He quickly removed the headphones. "Sorry."

"Your first patient is here, Dr. Phillips."

He glanced at his watch, and then at his appointment print-out. "My schedule shows an opening now."

"I guess the call center filled it last-minute."

"Chart?"

She shook her head.

"What's the patient's problem?"

"Wants some kind of referral to a specialist."

Maria avoided his suspicious gaze. She'd always been on top of her game as a medical assistant, yet today she was being vague and borderline incompetent. Maybe in his recent absence she'd forgotten his usual clinic procedure. He stood and clicked his tongue. If things didn't improve, he'd have to remind her of his preferred routine, *efficiency* being the key factor.

The nurse smiled when he passed her, and he gave her a suspicious glance. "Which exam room?"

"Four," she said, first staring at her feet, then quickly walking back to her cubicle.

"Did you at least get a name and age?"

She shrugged her shoulders. "I forgot. Sorry, Doctor." Then she scurried off.

He'd definitely have to get her back on track.

Hunter made a sharp tap on the exam door, and didn't wait for a response before opening it. He stepped inside but stopped short, his breath arresting in his throat. "Mandy?"

She sat tall, with one leg crossed, her fingertips balanced at both her sides on the exam table. Looking stunningly beautiful, and obviously dressed to please, she gazed tentatively at him, color rising on her cheeks.

"Hi," she said.

"What are you—"

She raised her hand before he could utter another sound. "First, I'm here on official business. I need a referral to Cardiology to arrange for cardiac ablation."

With her hair pulled back into a French twist, she looked sexy as all hell, and his mind was anywhere but at the office. However, though off balance, he followed her request, sat at the computer and brought up the referral screen. Finding it hard to concentrate, he couldn't even remember her date of birth without help. Together they filled in all the required information, and he had the opportunity to hear her entire medical history for the first time.

"So you hadn't been diagnosed when we were married?"

She shook her head. "Sometimes my heart would race, but I just assumed it was too much caffeine or stress or anxiety. It always settled down on its own. Until the first time I wound up in the ER." She furrowed her brows. "I should have told you, Hunter. Please forgive me. I'm sorry."

"I don't ever want to feel left out of your life again, Mandy." He stood inches from her, wanting more than anything to touch her. "If you don't trust me, how will you be able to love me?"

She shook her head, refusing to let her confidence slip away. "Life would be so much easier if it were all cut and dried the way we all seem to want it to be. But it's not like that. We're perplexing and confusing creatures. It's in our nature." His words finally sank in. "Did you just say something about me not being able to love you?"

He nodded.

"I *do* love you, Hunter. I swear."

"You have a strange way of showing it. We were together for six weeks and you never so much as hinted at any physical problem. I mean, I knew you seemed a bit frailer than before, and I sensed you'd changed. Hell, you even refused to have an EKG like everyone else in the project. But, come on, you should have clued me in to your condition."

"So you could treat me like my parents do?"

Her point was well taken. They stared at each other for that *touché* moment, and he decided to take another tack.

"Are you *sure* you want to go through with this procedure?"

She hopped off the exam table. "Knowing that I have Wolff-Parkinson-White syndrome, what would you advise, Doctor?"

He stood to meet her. "I'd advise having the ablation procedure as soon as possible."

In the high slinky heels she wore, she practically came eye to eye with him. "And since I trust your expertise completely, that's exactly what I intend to do."

He studied her unwavering eyes, searching for the most important answers and getting lost in their fresh blue promise.

"Can you forgive me?" she asked, knotting her hands.

Hell, she'd known him as a man who'd written off his own father and, when it came to having children with her, wouldn't bend. They'd divorced because of their differences over life plans. Of course she'd hesitate to tell him everything.

If he'd had any doubt about her sincerity, one more lingering look into her eyes answered his question. "I can do more than that," he said, taking her hands in his, feeling her cool fingers and ivory soft skin as if for the first time. "I can promise to always support your dreams, no matter how damn hard it will be on us." Half of his mouth smiled as he thought of something. "You want to know my secret?"

A curious smile stretched across her lips. "Of course. I want to know everything about you." She wove her fingers through his.

"For three years I kept it buried so deep I didn't even know that I never stopped loving you and wanted a second chance at being your husband."

She started to speak, but his hand flew up to stop her.

"Hear me out. Please. I was angry and bitter about marriage, and I thought it was for fools. Until I had Sophie I never wanted to be a father. Ever. And even then my first two weeks with her were pure drudgery. I felt stuck and trapped. If it hadn't been for you, I would have panicked and maybe even given up."

"I don't believe that. You would never abandon your niece."

"I was all she had, and it slowly dawned on me that I could be a different kind of father from my own. Of course I didn't realize any of this until I found you again. And then it took weeks to admit it to myself, and I never had the guts to tell a soul. Not even you."

Her eyes brightened with surprise. She held his hand tighter. "I'm stunned. Why didn't you tell me?"

He caressed her cheek and she leaned into his palm. "You weren't ready to hear it."

They gazed into each other's eyes as the moments stretched into seconds. He held her head and brushed her mouth with his own. She moistened her lips and kissed him softly. Inhaling her heavenly scent, he felt a kernel of joy sprout in his heart. His dreams were as near as her lips, and he never intended to let them out of his reach again.

"I love you, Hunter," she said.

He beamed. "Are you sure about that?"

"Yes."

"And I love you." He grinned again and gave her another kiss.

He took her into his arms and held her for several long moments. It felt incredible to be so close to the love of his life— the woman he never wanted to live without again.

She pulled away. "Hunter. What if, after all of this, I turn out to be a lousy mother?"

He laughed. "Not gonna happen. You know how to give and love with all your heart. Our babies will never doubt for a moment that they're loved."

Her eyes brightened with tears. "I'm glad you have more confidence in me than I have in myself."

"Can you forgive me for not always believing in you?"

"Yes." She dropped her head. "And since we're on a confession jag, you should know I've found a part-time PhD program right here in Los Angeles that will let me work at my own pace. Before I sign up, I want to run it by you. Get your opinion and see where you stand with it."

He curled her into his arms and breathed in the fresh fragrance of her hair. "You want my opinion?"

"Of course." Her arms wrapped around his back.

He was as near to heaven as he'd ever been, and hadn't Jack Howling said to grab life by the tail and hold on for a great ride? "How far will the commute be from my house?"

"What do you mean?"

"By the time you're admitted to the program, we'll be married and living together."

She stopped breathing for a moment, almost looking dazed, but life quickly sprang back into her ocean-blue eyes.

"Wait, wait, wait. Did you just ask me to marry you?"

"Oh, yeah." He smoothed his palm along her silky hair, tucking loose tendrils behind her ears. "In case you missed it. Will you marry me, Mandy?"

He prepared to catch her as the color drained from her face. But her cheeks quickly pinked up when she smiled. "Yes. Oh, yes."

With the last piece of the puzzle in place, Hunter took a deep

breath, realizing that for the first time in three years he felt
complete again. That beside the pure joy in his heart, a practical thought popped into his mind.

"While we're married and you're pursuing your advanced
degree, promise me no Urgent Care shifts?"

She laughed. "I can live with that."

He smiled, then grew serious. "And no more secrets."

She shook her head. "No more secrets," she repeated.

She scratched her upper lip and drew a breath. He had a
sneaky feeling an explanation was coming on.

"Okay. The Mending Hearts Program is going region-wide.
I'll need to take a few trips to train nurse practitioners at the
Oakland and San Diego Mercy Hospitals."

A confident smile stretched across his lips. "I can live with
that."

She nodded her head. "Me, too."

They cuddled in each other's arms for a few quiet moments,
until Mandy's head popped up. "So how long before I'll get that
appointment with Cardiology?"

"I'll arrange for you to get it ASAP. In fact, I'm thinking of
calling the electrophysiology lab personally after you leave."

A tap at the door reminded him he had a schedule to keep,
and patients to see. His nurse's missing efficiency had miraculously returned. "Dr. Phillips, your next patient is waiting in
room three." Her muffled voice came through the door. "The
chart is on your desk."

"I'll be right there." He lifted his brows and gazed happily
into Mandy's wide-eyed stare. "What are you doing for lunch?"

"I haven't made any plans."

He dug into his pocket and pulled out his keys, handing them
to Mandy. "I'll meet you at my house at noon sharp."

"Should I bring any particular food?"

"Here's a thought." He hoped she'd meet him at the door in nothing but those sexy shoes. "Skip the food. Why don't you surprise me with the rest?"

She chuckled.

"Any more questions?" he asked, pouring on the charm.

A sudden serious veil covered her face. "Will I be able to have a normal pregnancy after cardiac ablation?"

"Yes."

"How do you know?"

"Trust me, it was a long weekend. I've already checked it out. Truth is you've got an appointment with Dr. Mahmoud in Cardiology next week. I took the liberty to make that appointment for you."

"I thought you said no more secrets?"

He grinned. "It's only a secret if I don't tell. And, speaking of telling, I love you," he repeated, feeling as though he'd never said anything more important in his life.

"And I love you…with all my soul."

Her crystal-blue eyes sparkled with joy, and love was written all over her radiant face. He moved in for another world-class kiss.

Life was good.

A quiet tapping stopped them.

A sexy blush rose up Mandy's cheeks. "I'd better let you get back to your patients."

Regrettably he let go of her, knowing she'd be back in his arms again within a few hours. He grinned, planning to never let her out of his life again.

Mandy pecked him on the nose and sashayed on her sexy heels toward the door, stopping just long enough at the threshold to blow Hunter the most promising kiss of his lifetime.

# Passion. Power. Suspense.
# It's time to fall under the spell of Nora Roberts.

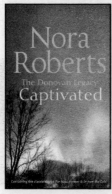
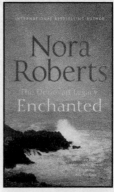
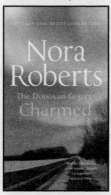
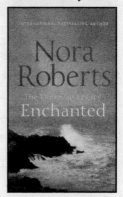

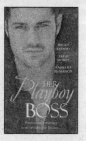

## 4 Books
### and a surprise gift!

We would like to take this opportunity to thank you for reading this Mills & Boon® book by offering you the chance to take FOUR more specially selected titles from the Medical™ series absolutely FREE! We're also making this offer to introduce you to the benefits of the Mills & Boon® Book Club™—

- ★ **FREE home delivery**
- ★ **FREE gifts and competitions**
- ★ **FREE monthly Newsletter**
- ★ **Exclusive Mills & Boon Book Club offers**
- ★ **Books available before they're in the shops**

Accepting these FREE books and gift places you under no obligation to buy, you may cancel at any time, even after receiving your free shipment. Simply complete your details below and return the entire page to the address below. You don't even need a stamp!

**YES!** Please send me 4 free Medical books and a surprise gift. I understand that unless you hear from me, I will receive 6 superb new titles every month for just £2.99 each, postage and packing free. I am under no obligation to purchase any books and may cancel my subscription at any time. The free books and gift will be mine to keep in any case.

M9ZEF

Ms/Mrs/Miss/Mr ........................................Initials...........................
**BLOCK CAPITALS PLEASE**

Surname.....................................................................................

Address...................................................................................

................................................................................................

.................................................Postcode ...............................

**Send this whole page to:**
**UK: FREEPOST CN81, Croydon, CR9 3WZ**